Life of John Milton

Richard Garnett

Contents

LIFE OF JOHN MILTON

BY

Richard Garnett

NOTE.

The number of miniature "Lives" of Milton is great; great also is the merit of some of them. With one exception, nevertheless, they are all dismissed to the shelf by the publication of Professor Masson's monumental and authoritative biography, without perpetual reference to which no satisfactory memoir can henceforth be composed. One recent biography has enjoyed this advantage. Its author, the late Mark Pattison, wanted neither this nor any other qualification except a keener sense of the importance of the religious and political controversies of Milton's time. His indifference to matters so momentous in Milton's own estimation has, in our opinion, vitiated his conception of his hero, who is represented as persistently yielding to party what was meant for mankind. We think, on the contrary, that such a mere man of letters as Pattison wishes that Milton had been, could never have produced a "Paradise Lost." If this view is well-founded, there is not only room but need for yet another miniature "Life of Milton," notwithstanding the intellectual subtlety and scholarly refinement which render Pattison's memorable. It should be noted that the recent German biography by Stern, if adding little to Professor Masson's facts, contributes much valuable literary illustration; and that Keighley's analysis of Milton's opinions occupies a position of its own, of which no subsequent biographical discoveries can deprive it. The present writer has further to express his deep obligations to Professor Masson for his great kindness in reading and remarking upon the proofs--not thereby rendering himself responsible for anything in these pages; and also to the helpful friend who has provided him with an index.

CHAPTER I.

Tohn Milton was born on December 9, 1608, when Shakespeare had lately produced "Antony and Cleopatra," when Bacon was writing his "Wisdom of the Ancients" and Ralegh his "History of the World," when the English Bible was hastening into print; when, nevertheless, in the opinion of most foreigners and many natives, England was intellectually unpolished, and her literature almost barbarous.

The preposterousness of this judgment as a whole must not blind us to the fragment of truth which it included. England's literature was, in many respects, very imperfect and chaotic. Her "singing masons" had already built her "roofs of gold"; Hooker and one or two other great prose-writers stood like towers: but the less exalted portions of the edifice were still half hewn. Some literatures, like the Latin and the French, rise gradually to the crest of their perfection; others, like the Greek and the English, place themselves almost from the first on their loftiest pinnacle, leaving vast gaps to be subsequently filled in. Homer was not less the supreme poet because history was for him literally an old song, because he would have lacked understanding for Plato and relish for Aristophanes. Nor were Shakespeare and the translators of the Bible less at the head of European literature because they must have failed as conspicuously as Homer would have failed in all things save those to which they had a call, which chanced to be the greatest. Literature, however, cannot remain isolated at such altitudes, it must expand or perish. As Homer's epic passed through Pindar and the lyrical poets into drama history and philosophy, continually fitting itself more and more to become an instrument in the ordinary affairs of life, so it was needful that English lettered discourse should become popular and pliant, a power in the State as well as in the study. The magnitude of the change, from the time when the palm of popularity decorated Sidney's "Arcadia" to that when it adorned

Defoe and Bunyan, would impress us even more powerfully if the interval were not engrossed by a colossal figure, the last of the old school in the erudite magnificence of his style in prose and verse; the first of the new, inasmuch as English poetry, hitherto romantic, became in his hands classical. This "splendid bridge from the old world to the new," as Gibbon has been called in a different connection, was John Milton: whose character and life-work, carefully analyzed, resolve themselves into pairs of equally vivid contrasts. A stern Puritan, he is none the less a freethinker in the highest and best sense of the term. The recipient of direct poetical inspiration in a measure vouchsafed to few, he notwithstanding studies to make himself a poet; writes little until no other occupation than writing remains to him; and, in general, while exhibiting even more than the usual confidence, shows less than the usual exultation and affluence of conscious genius. Professing to recognize his life's work in poetry, he nevertheless suffers himself to be diverted for many a long year into political and theological controversy, to the scandal and compassion of one of his most competent and attached biographers. Whether this biographer is right or wrong, is a most interesting subject for discussion. We deem him wrong, and shall not cease to reiterate that Milton would not have been Milton if he could have forgotten the citizen in the man of letters. Happy, at all events, it is that this and similar problems occupy in Milton's life the space which too frequently has to be spent upon the removal of misconception, or the refutation of calumny. Little of a sordid sort disturbs the sentiment of solemn reverence with which, more even than Shakespeare's, his life is approached by his countrymen; a feeling doubtless mainly due to the sacred nature of his principal theme, but equally merited by the religious consecration of his whole existence. It is the easier for the biographer to maintain this reverential attitude, inasmuch as the prayer of Agur has been fulfilled in him, he has been given neither poverty nor riches. He is not called upon to deal with an enormous mass of material, too extensive to arrange, yet too important to neglect. Nor is he, like Shakespeare's biographer, reduced to choose between the starvation of nescience and the windy diet of conjecture. If a humbling thought intrudes, it is how largely he is indebted to a devoted diligence he never could have emulated; how painfully Professor Masson's successors must resemble the Turk who builds his cabin out of Grecian or Roman ruins.

Milton's genealogy has taxed the zeal and acumen of many investigators. He himself merely claims a respectable ancestry (ex genere honesto). His nephew Phillips professed to have come upon the root of the family tree at Great Milton, in Oxfordshire, where tombs attested the residence of the clan, and tradition its proscription and impoverishment in the Wars of the Roses. Monuments, station, and confiscation have vanished before the scrutiny of the Rev. Joseph Hunter; it can only be safely concluded that Milton's ancestors dwelt in or near the village of Holton, by Shotover Forest, in Oxfordshire, and that their rank in life was probably that of yeomen. Notwithstanding Aubrey's statement that Milton's grandfather's name was John, Mr. Hyde Clarke's researches in the registers of the Scriveners' Company have proved that Mr. Hunter and Professor Masson were right in identifying him with Richard Milton, of Stanton St. John, near Holton; and Professor Masson has traced the family a generation further back to Henry Milton, whose will, dated November 21, 1558, attests a condition of plain comfort, nearer poverty than riches. Henry Milton's goods at his death were inventoried at L6 19s.; when his widow's will is proved, two years afterwards, the estimate is L7 4s. 4d. Richard, his son, is stated, but not proved, to have been an under-ranger of Shotover Forest. He appears to have married a widow named Jeffrey, whose maiden name had been Haughton, and who had some connection with a Cheshire family of station. He would also seem to have improved his circumstances by the match, which may account for the superior education of his son John, whose birth is fixed by an affidavit to 1562 or 1563. Aubrey, indeed, next to Phillips and Milton himself, the chief contemporary authority, says that he was for a time at Christ Church, Oxford--a statement in itself improbable, but slightly confirmed by his apparent acquaintance with Latin, and the family tradition that his course of life was diverted by a quarrel with his father. Queen Mary's stakes and faggots had not affected Richard Milton as they affected most Englishmen. Though churchwarden in 1582, he must have continued to adhere to the ancient faith, for he was twice fined for recusancy in 1601, which lends credit to the statement that his son was cast off by him for Protestantism. "Found him reading the Bible in his chamber," says Aubrey, who adds that the younger Milton never was a scrivener's apprentice; but this is shown to be an error by Mr. Hyde Clarke's discovery of his admission to the Scriveners' Company in 1599, where he is stated to have been apprentice to James Colborn. Colborn himself had been only four years in business, instead of the seven which would usually be required for an apprentice to serve out his indenture--which suggests that some formalities may have been dispensed with on account of John Milton's age. A scrivener was a kind of cross between an attorney and a law stationer, whose principal business was the preparation of deeds, "to be well and truly done after my learning, skill, and science," and with due regard to the interests of more exalted personages. "Neither for haste nor covetousness I shall take upon me to make any deed whereof I have not cunning, without good advice and information of counsel." Such a calling offered excellent opportunities for investments; and John Milton, a man of strict integrity and frugality, came to possess a "plentiful estate." Among his possessions was the house in Bread Street destroyed in the Great Fire. The tenement where the poet was born, being a shop, required a sign, for which he chose The Spread Eagle, either from the crest of such among the Miltons as had a right to bear arms, among whom he may have reckoned himself; or as the device of the Scriveners' Company. He had been married about 1600 to a lady whose name has been but lately ascertained to have been Sarah Jeffrey. John Milton the younger was the third of six children, only three of whom survived infancy. He grew up between a sister, Anne, several years older, and a brother, Christopher, seven years younger than himself.

Milton's birth and nurture were thus in the centre of London; but the London of that day had not half the population of the Liverpool of ours. Even now the fragrance of the hay in far-off meadows may be inhaled in Bread Street on a balmy summer's night; then the meadows were near the doors, and the undefiled sky was reflected by an unpolluted stream. There seems no reason to conclude that Milton, in his early boyhood, enjoyed any further opportunities of resort to rural scenery than the vicinity of London could afford; but if the city is his native element, natural beauty never appeals to him in vain. Yet the influences which moulded his childhood must have been rather moral and intellectual than merely natural:--

"The starlight smile of children, the sweet looks
Of women, the fair breast from which I fed,"
played a greater part in the education of this poet than

"The murmur of the unreposing brooks,
And the green light which, shifting overhead,

Some tangled bower of vines around me shed,
The shells on the sea-sand, and the wild flowers."

Paramount to all other influences must have been the character of his father,
a "mute" but by no means an "inglorious" Milton, the preface and foreshadowing
of the son. His great step in life had set the son the example from which the latter never swerved, and from him the younger Milton derived not only the independence of thought which was to lead him into moral and social heresy, and the
fidelity to principle which was to make him the Abdiel of the Commonwealth, but
no mean share of his poetical faculty also. His mastery of verbal harmony was but
a new phase of his father's mastery of music, which he himself recognizes as the
complement of his own poetical gift:--

"Ipse volens Phoebus se dispertire duobus,
Altera dona mihi, dedit altera dona parenti."

As a composer, the circumspect, and, as many no doubt thought prosaic scrivener, took rank among the best of his day. One of his compositions, now lost, was
rewarded with a gold medal by a Polish prince (Aubrey says the Landgrave of
Hesse), and he appears among the contributors to **The Triumphs of Oriana**, a set
of twenty-five madrigals composed in honour of Queen Elizabeth. "The Teares and
Lamentations of a Sorrowful Soule"--dolorous sacred songs, Professor Masson calls
them--were, according to their editor, the production of "famous artists," among
whom Byrd, Bull, Dowland, Orlando Gibbons, certainly figure, and three of them
were composed by the elder Milton. He also harmonized the Norwich and York
psalm tunes, which were adapted to six of the Psalms in Ravenscroft's Collection.
Such performance bespeaks not only musical accomplishment, but a refined nature;
and we may well believe that Milton's love of learning, as well as his love of music,
was hereditary in its origin, and fostered by his contact with his father. Aubrey
distinctly affirms that Milton's skill on the organ was directly imparted to him by
his father, and there would be nothing surprising if the first rudiments of knowledge were also instilled by him. Poetry he may have taught by precept, but the one
extant specimen of his Muse is enough to prove that he could never have taught it

by example.

We have therefore to picture Milton growing up in a narrow street amid a strict Puritan household, but not secluded from the influences of nature or uncheered by melodious recreations; and tenderly watched over by exemplary parents--a mother noted, he tells us, for her charities among her neighbours, and a father who had discerned his promise from the very first. Given this perception in the head of a religious household, it almost followed in that age that the future poet should receive the education of a divine. Happily, the sacerdotal caste had ceased to exist, and the education of a clergyman meant not that of a priest, but that of a scholar. Milton was instructed daily, he says, both at grammar schools and under private masters, "as my age would suffer," he adds, in acknowledgment of his father's considerateness. Like Disraeli two centuries afterwards (perhaps the single point of resemblance), he went for schooling to a Nonconformist in Essex, "who," says Aubrey, "cut his hair short." His own hair? or his pupil's? queries Biography. We boldly reply, Both. Undoubtedly Milton's hair is short in the miniature painted of him at the age of ten by, as is believed, Cornelius Jansen. A thoughtful little face, that of a well-nurtured, towardly boy; lacking the poetry and spirituality of the portrait of eleven years later, where the long hair flows down upon the ruff.

After leaving his Essex pedagogue, Milton came under the private tuition of Thomas Young, a Scotchman from St. Andrews, who afterwards rose to be master of Jesus College, Cambridge. It would appear from the elegies subsequently addressed to him by his pupil that he first taught Milton to write Latin verse. This instruction was no doubt intended to be preliminary to the youth's entrance at St. Paul's School, where he must have been admitted by 1620 at the latest.

At the time of Milton's entry, St. Paul's stood high among the schools of the metropolis, competing with Merchant Taylors', Westminster, and the now extinct St. Anthony's. The headmaster, Dr. Gill, was an admirable scholar, though, as Aubrey records, "he had his whipping fits." His fitful severity was probably more tolerable than the systematic cruelty of his predecessor Mulcaster (Spenser's schoolmaster when he presided over Merchant Taylors'), of whom Fuller approvingly records: "Atropos might be persuaded to pity as soon as he to pardon where he found just fault. The prayers of cockering mothers prevailed with him as much as the requests of indulgent fathers, rather increasing than mitigating his severity on their offending children." Milton's father, though by no means "cockering," would not have tolerated such discipline, and the passionate ardour with which Milton threw himself into the studious life of the school is the best proof that he was exempt from tyranny. "From the twelfth year of my age," he says, "I scarcely ever went from my lessons to bed before midnight." The ordinary school tasks cannot have exacted so much time from so gifted a boy: he must have read largely outside the regular curriculum, and probably he practised himself diligently in Latin verse. For this he would have the prompting, and perhaps the aid, of the younger Gill, assistant to his father, who, while at the University, had especially distinguished himself by his skill in versification. Gill must also have been a man of letters, affable and communicative, for Milton in after-years reminds him of their "almost constant conversations," and declares that he had never left his company without a manifest accession of literary knowledge. The Latin school exercises have perished, but two English productions of the period, paraphrases of Psalms executed at fifteen, remain to attest the boy's proficiency in contemporary English literature. Some of the unconscious borrowings attributed to him are probably mere coincidences, but there is still enough to evince acquaintance with "Sylvester, Spenser, Drummond, Drayton, Chaucer, Fairfax, and Buchanan." The literary merit of these versions seems to us to have been underrated. There may be no individual phrase beyond the compass of an apt and sensitive boy with a turn for verse-making; but the general tone is masculine and emphatic. There is not much to say, but what is said is delivered with a "large utterance," prophetic of the "os magna soniturum," and justifying his own report of his youthful promise:--"It was found that whether aught was imposed me by them that had the overlooking, or betaken to of mine own choice, in English or other tongue, prosing or versing, but chiefly by this latter, the style, by certain vital signs it had, was likely to live."

Among the incidents of Milton's life at St. Paul's School should not be forgotten his friendship with Charles Diodati, the son of a Genevese physician settled in England, whose father had been exiled from Italy for his Protestantism. A friendship memorable not only as Milton's tenderest and his first, but as one which quickened his instinctive love of Italian literature, enhanced the pleasure, if it did not suggest the undertaking, of his Italian pilgrimage, and doubtless helped to inspire the execration which he launched in after years against the slayers of the Vaudois.

The Italian language is named by him among three which, about the time of his migration to the University, he had added to the classical and the vernacular, the other two being French and Hebrew. It has been remarked, however, that his use of "Penseroso," incorrect both in orthography and signification, shows that prior to his visit to Italy he was unacquainted with the niceties of the language. He entered as "a lesser pensioner" at Christ's College, Cambridge, on February 12, 1625; the greatest poetic name in an University roll already including Spenser, and destined to include Dryden, Gray, Wordsworth, Coleridge, Byron, and Tennyson. Why Oxford was not preferred has been much debated. The father may have taken advice from the younger Gill, whose Liberalism had got him into trouble at that University. He may also have been unwilling to place his son in the neighbourhood of his estranged relatives. Shortly before Milton's matriculation his sister had married Mr. Edward Phillips, of the office of the Clerk of the Crown, now abolished, then charged with the issue of Parliamentary and judicial writs. From this marriage were to spring the young men who were to find an instructor in Milton, as he in one of them a biographer.

The external aspect of Milton's Cambridge is probably not ill represented by Lyne's coloured map of half a century earlier, now exhibited in the King's Library at the British Museum. Piles of stately architecture, from King's College Chapel downward, tower all about, over narrow, tortuous, pebble-paved streets, bordered with diminutive, white-fronted, red-tiled dwellings, mere dolls' houses in comparison. So modest, however, is the chartographer's standard, that a flowery Latin inscription assures the men of Cambridge they need but divert Trumpington Brook into Clare Ditch to render their town as elegant as any in the universe. Sheep and swine perambulate the environs, and green spaces are interspersed among the colleges, sparsely set with trees, so pollarded as to justify Milton's taunt when in an ill-humour with his university:--

"Nuda nec arva placent, umbrasque negantia molles,
Quam male Phoebicolis convenit ille locus!"

His own college stands conspicuous at the meeting of three ways, aptly suggestive of Hecate and infernal things. Its spiritual and intellectual physiognomy, and that of the university in general, must be learned from the exhaustive pages of Professor Masson. A book unpublished when he wrote, Ball's life of Dr. John Preston, Master of Emmanuel, vestige of an entire continent of submerged Puritanism, also contributes much to the appreciation of the place and time. We can here but briefly characterize the University as an institution undergoing modification, rather by the decay of the old than by the intrusion of the new. The revolution by which mathematics became the principal instrument of culture was still to be deferred forty years. Milton, who tells us that he delighted in mathematics, might have been nearly ignorant of that subject if he pleased, and hardly could become proficient in it by the help of his Alma Mater. The scholastic philosophy, however, still reigned. But even here tradition was shaky and undermined; and in matters of discipline the rigid code which nominally governed the University was practically much relaxed. The teaching staff was respectable in character and ability, including many future bishops. But while the academical credentials of the tutors were unimpeachable, perhaps not one among them all could show a commission from the Spirit. No one then at Cambridge seems to have been in the least degree capable of arousing enthusiasm. It might not indeed have been easy for a Newman or a Green to captivate the independent soul of Milton, even at this susceptible period of his life; failing any approach to such external influence, he would be likely to leave Cambridge the same man as he entered it. Ere, indeed, he had completed a year's residence, his studies were interrupted by a temporary rupture with the University, probably attributable to his having been at first placed under an uncongenial tutor. William Chappell was an Arminian and a tool of Laud, who afterwards procured him preferment in Ireland, and, as Professor Masson judges from his treatise on homiletics, "a man of dry, meagre nature." His relations with such a pupil could not well be harmonious; and Aubrey charges him with unkindness, a vague accusation rendered tangible by the interlined gloss, "Whipt him." Hence the legend, so dear to Johnson, that Milton was the last man to be flogged at college. But Aubrey can hardly mean anything more than that Chappell on some occasion struck or beat his pupil, and this interpretation is supported by Milton's verses to Diodati, written in the spring of 1626, in which, while acknowledging that he had been directed to withdraw from Cambridge ("nec dudum vetiti me laris angit amor") he expresses his intention of speedily returning:--

"Stat quoque juncosas Cami remeare paludes,
Atque iterum raucae murmur adire scholae."

A short rustication would be just the notice the University would be likely to take of the conduct of a pupil who had been engaged in a scuffle with his tutor, in which the fault was not wholly or chiefly his. Formal corporal punishment would have rendered rustication unnecessary. That Milton was not thought wholly in the wrong appears from his not having been mulcted of a term's residence, his absence notwithstanding, and from the still more significant fact that Chappell lost his pupil. His successor was Nathaniel Tovey, in whom his patroness, the Countess of Bedford, had discerned "excellent talent." What Milton thought of him there is nothing to show.

This temporary interruption of the smoothness of Milton's University life occurred, as has been seen, quite early in its course. Had it indeed implied a stigma upon him or the University, the blot would in either case have been effaced by the perfect regularity of his subsequent career. He went steadily through the academic course, which to attain the degree of Master of Arts, then required seven years' residence. He graduated as Bachelor at the proper time, March, 1629, and proceeded Master in July, 1632. His general relations with the University during the period may be gathered partly from his own account in after years, when perhaps he in some degree "confounded the present feelings with the past," partly from a remarkable passage in one of his academical exercises, fortunately preserved to us, the importance of which was first discerned by his editor and biographer Mitford. Professor Masson, however, ascertained the date, which is all important. We must picture Milton "affable, erect, and manly," as Wood describes him, speaking from a low pulpit in the hall of Christ's College, to an audience of various standing, from grave doctors to skittish undergraduates, with most of whom he was in daily intercourse. The term is the summer of 1628, about nine months before his graduation; the words were Latin, but we resort to the version of Professor Masson:--

"Then also there drew and invited me, in no ordinary degree, to
undertake this part your very recently discovered graciousness to
me. For when, some few months ago, I was about to perform an

oratorical office before you, and was under the impression that
any lucubrations whatsoever of mine would be the reverse of
agreeable to you, and would have more merciful judges in Aeacus
and Minos than almost any of you would prove, truly, beyond my
fancy, beyond my hope if I had any, they were, as I heard, nay, as
I myself felt, received with the not ordinary applause of
all--yea, of those who at other times were, on account of
disagreements in our studies, altogether of an angry and
unfriendly spirit towards me. A generous mode of exercising
rivalry this, and not unworthy of a royal breast, if, when
friendship itself is wont often to misconstrue much that is
blamelessly done, yet then sharp and hostile enmity did not grudge
to interpret much that was perchance erroneous, and not a little,
doubtless, that was unskilfully said, more clemently than I
merited."

It is sufficiently manifest from this that after two years' residence Milton had
incurred much anger and unpopularity "on account of disagreements in our studies," which can scarcely mean anything else than his disapprobation of the University system. Notwithstanding this he had been received on a former occasion with
unexpected favour, and on the present is able to say, "I triumph as one placed among
the stars that so many men, eminent for erudition, and nearly the whole University have flocked hither." We have thus a miniature history of Milton's connection
with his Alma Mater. We see him giving offence by the freedom of his strictures on
the established practices, and misliking them so much as to write in 1642, "Which
[University] as in the time of her better health and mine own younger judgment, I
never greatly admired, so now much less." But, on the other hand, we see his intellectual revolt overlooked on account of his unimpeachable conduct and his brilliant
talents, and himself selected to represent his college on an occasion when an able
representative was indispensable. Cambridge had all imaginable complacency in
the scholar, it was towards the reformer that she assumed, as afterwards towards
Wordsworth, the attitude of

"Blind Authority beating with his staff
The child that would have led him."

The University and Milton made a practical covenant like Frederick the Great and his subjects: she did what she pleased, and he thought what he pleased. In sharp contrast with his failure to influence her educational methods is "that more than ordinary respect which I found above any of my equals at the hands of those courteous and learned men, the Fellows of that College wherein I spent seven years; who, at my parting, after I had taken two degrees, as the manner is, signified many ways how much better it would content them that I would stay; as by many letters full of kindness and loving respect, both before that time and long after, I was assured of their singular good affection toward me." It may be added here that his comeliness and his chastity gained him the appellation of "Lady" from his fellow collegians: and the rooms at Christ's alleged to have been his are still pointed out as deserving the veneration of poets in any event; for whether Milton sacrificed to Apollo in them or not, it is certain that in them Wordsworth sacrificed to Bacchus.

For Milton's own sake and ours his departure from the University was the best thing that could have happened to him. It saved him from wasting his time in instructing others when he ought to be instructing himself. From the point of view of advantage to the University, it is perhaps the most signal instance of the mischief of strictly clerical fellowships, now happily things of the past. Only one fellowship at Christ's was tenable by a layman: to continue in academical society, therefore, he must have taken orders. Such had been his intention when he first repaired to Cambridge, but the young man of twenty-three saw many things differently from the boy of sixteen. The service of God was still as much as ever the aim of his existence, but he now thought that not all service was church service. How far he had become consciously alienated from the Church's creed it is difficult to say. He was able, at all events, to subscribe the Articles on taking his degree, and no trace of Arianism appears in his writings for many years. As late as 1641 he speaks of "the tri-personal Deity." Curiously enough, indeed, the ecclesiastical freethought of the day was then almost entirely confined to moderate Royalists, Hales, Chillingworth, Falkland. But he must have disapproved of the Church's discipline, for he disapproved of all discipline. He would not put himself in the position of those

Irish clergymen whom Strafford frightened out of their conscientious convictions by reminding them of their canonical obedience. This was undoubtedly what he meant when he afterwards wrote: "Perceiving that he who would take orders must subscribe slave." Speaking of himself a little further on as "Church-outed by the prelates," he implies that he would not have refused orders if he could have had them on his own terms. As regarded Milton personally this attitude was reasonable, he had a right to feel himself above the restraints of mere formularies; but he spoke unadvisedly if he meant to contend that a priest should be invested with the freedom of a Prophet. His words, however, must be taken in connection with the peculiar circumstances of the time. It was an era of High Church reaction, which was fast becoming a shameful persecution. The two moderate prelates, Abbot and Williams, had for years been in disgrace, and the Church was ruled by the well-meaning, but sour, despotic, meddlesome bigot whom wise King James long refused to make a bishop because "he could not see when matters were well." But if Laud was infatuated as a statesman, he was astute as a manager; he had the Church completely under his control, he was fast filling it with his partisans and creatures, he was working it for every end which Milton most abhorred, and was, in particular, allying it with a king who in 1632 had governed three years without a Parliament. The mere thought that he must call this hierarch his Father in God, the mere foresight that he might probably come into collision with him, and that if he did his must be the fate of the earthen vessel, would alone have sufficed to deter Milton from entering the Church.

Even so resolute a spirit as Milton's could hardly contemplate the relinquishment of every definite calling in life without misgiving, and his friends could hardly let it pass without remonstrance. There exists in his hand the draft of a letter of reply to the verbal admonition of some well-wisher, to whom he evidently feels that he owes deference. His friend seems to have thought that he was yielding to the allurements of aimless study, neglecting to return as service what he had absorbed as knowledge. Milton pleads that his motive must be higher than the love of lettered ease, for that alone could never overcome the incentives that urge him to action. "Why should not all the hopes that forward youth and vanity are afledge with, together with gain, pride, and ambition, call me forward more powerfully than a poor, regardless, and unprofitable sin of curiosity should be able to withhold?" And what of the "desire of honour and repute and immortal fame seated in the breast of every true scholar?" That his correspondent may the better understand him, he encloses a "Petrarchean sonnet," recently composed, on his twenty-third birthday, not one of his best, but precious as the first of his frequent reckonings with himself:--

"How soon hath Time, the subtle thief of youth,
Stolen on his wing my three-and-twentieth year!
My hasting days fly on with full career;
But my late spring no bud or blossom shew'th.
Perhaps my semblance might deceive the truth,
That I to manhood am arrived so near;
And inward ripeness doth much less appear,
Than some more timely-happy spirits indu'th.
Yet be it less or more, or soon or slow,
It shall be still in strictest measure even
To that same lot, however mean or high,
Towards which Time leads me, and the Will of Heaven.
All is, if I have grace to use it so,
As ever in my great Taskmaster's eye."

The poetical temperament is especially liable to misgiving and despondency, and from this Milton evidently was not exempt. Yet he is the same Milton who proclaimed a quarter of a century afterwards--

"I argue not
Against Heaven's hand or will, nor bate a jot
Of heart or hope; but still bear up and steer
Right onward."

There is something very fine in the steady resolution with which, after so fully admitting to himself that his promise is yet unfulfilled, and that appearances are against him, he recurs to his purpose, frankly owning the while that the gift he craves is Heaven's, and his only the application. He had received a lesson against over-confidence in the failure of his solitary effort up to this time to achieve a work on a large scale. To the eighth and last stanza of his poem, "The Passion of Christ," is appended the note: "This subject the author finding to be above the years he had when he wrote it, and nothing satisfied with what was begun, left it unfinished." It nevertheless begins nobly, but soon deviates into conceits, bespeaking a fatigued imagination. The "Hymn on the Nativity," on the other hand, begins with two stanzas of far-fetched prettiness, and goes on ringing and thundering through strophes of ever-increasing grandeur, until the sweetness of Virgin and Child seem in danger of being swallowed up in the glory of Christianity; when suddenly, by an exquisite turn, the poet sinks back into his original key, and finally harmonizes his strain by the divine repose of concluding picture worthy of Correggio:--

> "But see, the Virgin blest
> Hath laid the Babe to rest;
> Time is our tedious song should here have ending;
> Heaven's youngest-teemed star
> Hath fixed her polished car,
> Her sleeping Lord with handmaid lamp attending;
> And all about the courtly stable
> Bright harnessed Angels sit in order serviceable."

In some degree this magnificent composition loses force in our day from its discordance with modern sentiment. We look upon religions as members of the same family, and are more interested in their resemblances than their antagonisms. Moloch and Dagon themselves appear no longer as incarnate fiends, but as the spiritual counterparts of antediluvian monsters; and Milton's treatment of the Olympian deities jars upon us who remember his obligations to them. If the most Hebrew of modern poets, he still owed more to Greece than to Palestine. How living a thing Greek mythology was to him from his earliest years appears from his college vacation exercise of 1628, where there are lines which, if one did not know to be Milton's, one would declare to be Keats's. Among his other compositions by the time of his quitting Cambridge are to be named the superb verses, "At a Solemn Music," perhaps the most perfect expression of his ideal of song; the pretty but over fanciful lines, "On a fair Infant dying of a cough;" and the famous panegyric of Shakespeare, a fancy made impressive by dignity and sonority of utterance.

With such earnest of a true vocation, Milton betook himself to retirement at Horton, a village between Colnbrook and Datchet, in the south-eastern corner of Buckinghamshire, county of nightingales, where his father had settled himself on his retirement from business. This retreat of the elder Milton may be supposed to have taken place in 1632, for in that year he took his clerk into partnership, probably devolving the larger part of the business upon him. But it may have been earlier, for in 1626 Milton tells Diodati--

"Nos quoque lucus habet vicina consitus ulmo,
Atque suburbani nobilis umbra loci."

And in a college declamation, which cannot have been later than 1632, he "calls to witness the groves and rivers, and the beloved village elms, under which in the last past summer I remember having had supreme delight with the Muses, when I too, among rural scenes and remote forests, seemed as if I could have grown and vegetated through a hidden eternity."

CHAPTER II.

Doctor Johnson deemed "the knowledge of nature half the task of a poet," but not until he had written all his poetry did he repair to the Highlands. Milton allows natural science and the observation of the picturesque no place among the elements of a poetical self-education, and his practice differs entirely from that which would in our day be adopted by an aspirant happy in equal leisure. Such an one would probably have seen no inconsiderable portion of the globe ere he could resolve to bury himself in a tiny hamlet for five years. The poems which Milton composed at Horton owe so much of their beauty to his country residence as to convict him of error in attaching no more importance to the influences of scenery. But this very excellence suggests that the spell of scenery need not be exactly proportioned to its grandeur.

The beauties of Horton are characterized by Professor Masson as those of "rich, teeming, verdurous flat, charming by its appearance of plenty, and by the goodly show of wood along the fields and pastures, in the nooks where the houses nestle, and everywhere in all directions to the sky-bound verge of the landscape." He also notices "the canal-like abundance and distribution of water. There are rivulets brimming through the meadows among rushes and water-plants; and by the very sides of the ways, in lieu of ditches, there are slow runnels, in which one can see the minnows swimming." The distant keep of Windsor, "bosomed high in tufted trees," is the only visible object that appeals to the imagination, or speaks of anything outside of rural peace and contentment. Milton's house, as Todd was informed by the vicar of the parish, stood till about 1798. If so, however, it is very remarkable that the writer of an account of Horton in the **Gentleman's Magazine** for August, 1791, who speaks of Milton with veneration, and transcribes his mother's epitaph, does not allude to the existence of his house. Its site is traditionally identified with that of Berkyn Manor, near the church, and an old pigeon-house is asserted to be a remnant of the original building. The elder Milton was no doubt merely the tenant; his landlord is said to have been the Earl of Bridgewater, but as there is no evidence of the Earl having possessed property in Horton, the statement may be merely an inference from Milton's poetical connection with the family. If not Bridgewater, the landlord was probably Bulstrode, the lord of the manor, and chief personage in the village. The Miltons still kept a footing in the metropolis. Christopher Milton, on his admission to the Inner Temple in September, 1632, is described as second son of John Milton of London, and subsequent legal proceedings disclose that the father, with the aid of his partner, was still doing business as a scrivener in 1637. It may be guessed that the veteran cit would not be sorry to find himself occasionally back in town. What with social exclusiveness, political and religious controversy, and uncongeniality of tastes, the Miltons' country circle of acquaintance was probably narrow. After five years of country life the younger Milton at all events thought seriously of taking refuge in an Inn of Court, "wherever there is a pleasant and shady walk," and tells Diodati, "Where I am now I live obscurely and in a cramped manner." He had only just made the acquaintance of his distinguished neighbour, Sir Henry Wotton, Provost of Eton, by the beginning of 1638, though it appears that he was previously acquainted with John Hales.

Milton's five years at Horton were nevertheless the happiest of his life. It must have been an unspeakable relief to him to be at length emancipated from compulsory exercises, and to build up his mind without nod or beck from any quarter. For these blessings he was chiefly indebted to his father, whose industry and prudence had procured his independence and his rural retirement, and whose tender indulgence and noble confidence dispensed him from what most would have deemed the reasonable condition that he should at least earn his own living. "I will not," he exclaims to his father, "praise thee for thy fulfilment of the ordinary duties of a parent, my debt is heavier (me poscunt majora). Thou hast neither made me a merchant nor a barrister":--

"Neque enim, pater, ire jubebas
Qua via lata patet, qua pronior area lucri,
Certaque condendi fulget spes aurea nummi:

Nec rapis ad leges, male custoditaque gentis
Jura, nec insulsis damnas clamoribus aures."

The stroke at the subserviency of the lawyers to the Crown (male custodita jura gentis) would be appreciated by the elder Milton, nor can we doubt that the old Puritan fully approved his son's resilience from a church denied by Arminianism and prelacy. He would not so easily understand the dedication of a life to poetry, and the poem from which the above citation is taken seems to have been partly composed to smooth his repugnance away. He was soon to have stronger proofs that his son had not mistaken his vocation: it would be pleasant to be assured that the old man was capable of valuing "Comus" and "Lycidas" at their worth. The circumstances under which "Comus" was produced, and its subsequent publication with the extorted consent of the author, show that Milton did not wholly want encouragement and sympathy. The insertion of his lines on Shakespeare in the Second Folio (1632) also denotes some reputation as a wit. In the main, however, remote from urban circles and literary cliques, with few correspondents and no second self in sweetheart or friend, he must have led a solitary intellectual life, alone with his great ambition, and probably pitied by his acquaintance. "The world," says Emerson to the Poet, "is full of renunciations and apprenticeships, and this is thine; thou must pass for a fool and a churl for a long season. This is the screen and sheath in which Pan has protected his well-beloved flower." The special nature of Milton's studies cannot now be exactly ascertained. Of his manner of studying he informs Diodati, "No delay, no rest, no care or thought almost of anything holds me aside until I reach the end I am making for, and round off, as it were, some great period of my studies." Of his object he says: "God has instilled into me, at all events, a vehement love of the beautiful. Not with so much labour is Ceres said to have sought Proserpine as I am wont day and night to seek for the idea of the beautiful through all the forms and faces of things, and to follow it leading me on as with certain assured traces." We may be sure that he read the classics of all the languages which he understood. His copies of Euripides, Pindar, Aratus, and Lycophron, are, or have been recently, extant, with marginal notes, proving that he weighed what he read. A commonplace book contains copious extracts from historians, and he tells Diodati that he has read Greek history to the fall of Constantinople. He speaks of having occasionally repaired to London for instruction in mathematics and music. His own programme, promulgated eight years later, but without doubt perfectly appropriate to his Horton period, names before all else--"Devout prayer to the Holy Spirit, that can enrich with all utterance and knowledge, and send out His Seraphim with the hallowed fire of His altar, to touch and purify the lips of whom He pleases. To this must be added select reading, steady observation, and insight into all seemly and generous arts and affairs, till which in some measure be compassed, I refuse not to sustain this expectation." This is not the ideal of a mere scholar, as Mark Paulson thinks he at one time was, and would wish him to have remained. "Affairs" are placed fully on a level with "arts." Milton was kept from politics in his youth, not by any notion of their incompatibility with poetry; but by the more cogent arguments at their command "under whose inquisitious and tyrannical duncery no free and splendid wit can flourish."

Milton's poetical development is, in many respects, exceptional. Most poets would no doubt, in theory, agree with Landor, "febriculis non indicari vires, impatientiam ab ignorantia non differre," but their faith will not be proved by lack of works, as Landor's precept and example require. He, who like Milton lisps in numbers usually sings freely in adolescence; he who is really visited by a true inspiration generally depends on mood rather than on circumstance. Milton, on the other hand, until fairly embarked on his great epic, was comparatively an unproductive, and literally an occasional poet. Most of his pieces, whether English or Latin, owe their existence to some impulse from without: "Comus" to the solicitation of a patron, "Lycidas" to the death of a friend. The "Allegro" and the "Penseroso" seem almost the only two written at the urgency of an internal impulse; and perhaps, if we knew their history, we should discover that they too were prompted by extraneous suggestion or provoked into being by accident. Such is the way with Court poets like Dryden and Claudian; it is unlike the usual procedure of Milton's spiritual kindred. Byron, Shelley, Tennyson, write incessantly; whatever care they may bestow upon composition, the impulse to produce is never absent. With Milton it is commonly dormant or ineffectual; he is always studying, but the fertility of his mind bears no apparent proportion to the pains devoted to its cultivation. He is not, like Wordsworth, labouring at a great work whose secret progress fills him with a majestic confidence; or, like Coleridge, dreaming of works which he lacks the energy to undertake; or, save once, does he seem to have felt with Keats:--

"Fears that I may cease to be
Before my pen has gleaned my teeming brain,
Before that books, in high piled charactery,
Hold in rich garners the full ripened grain."

He neither writes nor wishes to write; he simply studies, piling up the wood on the altar, and conscious of the power to call down fire from Heaven when he will. There is something sublime in this assured confidence; yet its wisdom is less evident than its grandeur. "No man," says Shelley, "can say, 'I will compose poetry.'" If he cannot say this of himself to-day, still less can he say it of himself to-morrow. He cannot tell whether the illusions of youth will forsake him wholly; whether the joy of creation will cease to thrill; what unpropitious blight he may encounter in an enemy or a creditor, or harbour in an uncongenial mate. Milton, no doubt, entirely meant what he said when he told Diodati: "I am letting my wings grow and preparing to fly, but my Pegasus has not yet feathers enough to soar aloft in the fields of air." But the danger of this protracted preparation was shown by his narrow escape from poetical shipwreck when the duty of the patriot became paramount to that of the poet. The Civil War confounded his anticipations of leisurely composition, and but for the disguised blessing of his blindness, the mountain of his attainment might have been Pisgah rather than Parnassus.

It is in keeping with the infrequency of Milton's moods of overmastering inspiration, and the strength of will which enabled him to write steadily or abstain from writing at all, that his early compositions should be, in general, so much more correct than those of other English poets of the first rank. The childish bombast of "Titus Andronicus," the commonplace of Wordsworth, the frequent inanity of the youthful Coleridge and the youthful Byron, Shelley's extravagance, Keats's cockneyism, Tennyson's mawkishness, find no counterpart in Milton's early compositions. All these great writers, though the span of some of them was but short, lived long enough to blush for much of what they had in the days of their ignorance taken for poetry. The mature Milton had no cause to be ashamed of anything written by the immature Milton, reasonable allowance being made for the inevitable infection of contemporary false taste. As a general rule, the youthful exuberance of a Shakespeare would be a better sign; faults, no less than beauties, often indicate the richness of the soil. But Milton was born to confute established opinions. Among other divergencies from usage, he was at this time a rare example of an English poet whose faculty was, in large measure, to be estimated by his essays in Latin verse. England had up to this time produced no distinguished Latin poet, though Scotland had: and had Milton's Latin poems been accessible, they would certainly have occupied a larger place in the estimation of his contemporaries than his English compositions. Even now they contribute no trifling addition to his fame, though they cannot, even as exercises, be placed in the highest rank. There are two roads to excellence in Latin verse--to write it as a scholar, or to write it as a Roman. England has once, and only once, produced a poet so entirely imbued with the Roman spirit that Latin seemed to come to him like the language of some prior state of existence, rather remembered than learned. Landor's Latin verse is hence greatly superior to Milton's, not, perhaps, in scholarly elegance, but in absolute vitality. It would be poor praise to commend it for fidelity to the antique, for it is the antique. Milton stands at the head of the numerous class who, not being actually born Romans, have all but made themselves so. "With a great sum obtained I this freedom." His Latin compositions are delightful, but precisely from the qualities least characteristic of his genius as an English poet. Sublimity and imagination are infrequent; what we have most commonly to admire are grace, ease, polish, and felicitous phrases rather concise in expression than weighty with matter. Of these merits the elegies to his friend Diodati, and the lines addressed to his father and to Manso, are admirable examples. The "Epitaphium Damonis" is in a higher strain, and we shall have to recur to it.

Except for his formal incorporation with the University of Oxford, by proceeding M.A. there in 1635, and the death of his mother on April 3, 1637, Milton's life during his residence at Horton, as known to us, is entirely in his writings. These comprise the "Sonnet to the Nightingale," "L'Allegro," "Il Penseroso," all probably written in 1633; "Arcades," probably, and "Comus" certainly written in 1634; "Lycidas" in 1637. The first three only are, or seem to be, spontaneous overflowings of the poetic mind: the others are composed in response to external invitations, and in two instances it is these which stand highest in poetic desert. Before entering on any criticism, it will be convenient to state the originating circumstances of each piece.

"Arcades" and "Comus" both owe their existence to the musician Henry Lawes, unless the elder Milton's tenancy of his house from the Earl of Bridgewater can be accepted as a fact. Both were written for the Bridgewater family, and if Milton felt no special devotion to this house, his only motive could have been to aid the musical performance of his friend Henry Lawes, whose music is discommended by Burney, but who, Milton declares:

"First taught our English music how to span
Words with just note and accent."

Masques were then the order of the day, especially after the splendid exhibition of the Inns of Court in honour of the King and Queen, February, 1634. Lawes, as a Court musician, took a leading part in this representation, and became in request on similar occasions. The person intended to be honoured by the "Arcades" was the dowager Countess of Derby, mother-in-law of the Earl of Bridgewater, whose father, Lord Keeper Egerton, she had married in 1600. The aged lady, to whom more than forty years before Spenser had dedicated his "Teares of the Muses," and who had ever since been an object of poetic flattery and homage, lived at Harefield, about four miles from Uxbridge; and there the "Arcades" were exhibited, probably in 1634. Milton's melodious verses were only one feature in a more ample entertainment. That they pleased we may be sure, for we find him shortly afterwards engaged on a similar undertaking of much greater importance, commissioned by the Bridgewater family. In those days Milton had no more of the Puritanic aversion to the theatre--

"Then to the well-trod stage anon,
If Jonson's learned sock be on,
Or sweetest Shakespeare, Fancy's child,
Warble his native wood-notes wild,"
than to the pomps and solemnities of cathedral ritual:--

"But let my due feet never fail
To walk the studious cloisters pale,
And love the high-embowed roof,
With antique pillars massy proof,
And storied windows richly dight,
Casting a dim religious light:
There let the pealing organ blow,
To the full-voic'd quire below,
In service high and anthems clear,
As may with sweetness through mine ear
Dissolve me into ecstacies,
And bring all heaven before mine eyes."

He therefore readily fell in with Lawes's proposal to write a masque to celebrate Lord Bridgewater's assumption of the Lord Presidency of the Welsh Marches. The Earl had entered upon the office in October, 1633, and "Comus" was written some time between this and the following September. Singular coincidences frequently linked Milton's fate with the north-west Midlands, from which his grandmother's family and his brother-in-law and his third wife sprung, whither the latter retired, where his friend Diodati lived, and his friend King died, and where now the greatest of his early works was to be represented in the time-hallowed precincts of Ludlow Castle, where it was performed on Michaelmas night, in 1634. If, as we should like to think, he was himself present, the scene must have enriched his memory and his mind. The castle--in which Prince Arthur had spent with his Spanish bride the six months of life which alone remained to him, in which eighteen years before the performance Charles the First had been installed Prince of Wales with extraordinary magnificence, and which, curiously enough, was to be the residence of the Cavalier poet, Butler--would be a place of resort for English tourists, if it adorned any country but their own. The dismantled keep is still an imposing object, lowering from a steep hill around whose base the curving Teme alternately boils and gushes with tumultuous speed. The scene within must have realized the lines in the "Allegro ":

"Pomp, and feast, and revelry,
Mask and antique pageantry,
Where throngs of knights and barons bold,
In weeds of peace high triumphs hold,
With store of ladies, whose bright eyes
Rain influence."

Lawes himself acted the attendant Spirit, the Lady and the Brothers were per-formed by Lord Bridgewater's youthful children, whose own nocturnal bewilder-ment in Haywood Forest, could we trust a tradition, doubted by the critics, but supported by the choice of the neighbourhood of Severn as the scene of the drama, had suggested his theme to Milton. He is evidently indebted for many incidents and ideas to Peele's "Old Wives' Tale," and the "Comus" of Erycius Puteanus; but there is little morality in the former production and little fancy in the latter. The peculiar blending of the highest morality with the noblest imagination is as much Milton's own as the incomparable diction. "I," wrote Sir Henry Wootton on receiving a copy of the anonymous edition printed by Lawes in 1637, "should much commend the tragical part if the lyrical did not ravish me with a certain Dorique delicacy in your songs and odes, whereunto I must plainly confess to have seen yet nothing parallel in our language." "Although not openly acknowledged by the author," says Lawes in his apology for printing prefixed to the poem, "it is a legitimate offspring, so lovely and so much desired that the often copying of it hath tired my pen to give my several friends satisfaction, and brought me to a necessity of producing it to the public view." The publication is anonymous, and bears no mark of Milton's partici-pation except a motto, which none but the author could have selected, intimating a fear that publication is premature. The title is simply "A Maske presented at Ludlow Castle," nor did the piece receive the name of "Comus" until after Milton's death.

It has been remarked that one of the most characteristic traits of Milton's ge-nius, until he laid hand to "Paradise Lost," is the dependence of his activity upon promptings from without. "Comus" once off his mind, he gives no sign of poetical life for three years, nor would have given any then but for the inaccurate chart or unskilful seamanship which proved fatal to his friend Edward King, August 10, 1637. King, a Fellow of Milton's college, had left Chester, on a voyage to Ireland, in the stillest summer weather:--

"The air was calm, and on the level brine
Sleek Panope and all her sisters played."

Suddenly the vessel struck on a rock, foundered, and all on board perished except some few who escaped in a boat. Of King it was reported that he refused to save himself, and sank to the abyss with hands folded in prayer. Great sympathy was excited among his friends at Cambridge, enough at least to evoke a volume of thirty-six elegies in various languages, but not enough to inspire any of the contributors, except Milton, with a poetical thought, while many are so ridiculous that quotation would be an affront to King's memory. But the thirty-sixth is "Lycidas." The original manuscript remains, and is dated in November. Of the elegy's relation to Milton's biography it may be said that it sums up the two influences which had been chiefly moulding his mind of late years, the natural influences of which he had been the passive recipient during his residence at Horton, and the political and theological passion with which he was becoming more and more inspired by the circumstances of the time. By 1637 the country had been eight years without a parliament, and the persecution of Puritans had attained its acme. In that year Laud's new Episcopalian service book was forced, or rather was attempted to be forced, upon Scotland; Prynne lost his ears; and Bishop Williams was fined eighteen thousand pounds and ordered to be imprisoned during the King's pleasure. Hence the striking, if incongruous, introduction of "The pilot of the Galilean lake," to bewail, in the character of a shepherd, the drowned swain in conjunction with Triton, Hippotades, and Camus. "The author," wrote Milton afterwards, "by occasion, foretells the ruin of the corrupted clergy, then in their height." It was a Parthian dart, for the volume was printed at the University Press in 1638, probably a little before his departure for Italy.

The "Penseroso" and the "Allegro," notwithstanding that each piece is the antithesis of the other, are complementary rather than contrary, and may be, in a sense, regarded as one poem, whose theme is the praise of the reasonable life. It resembles one of those pictures in which the effect is gained by contrasted masses of light and shade, but each is more nicely mellowed and interfused with the qualities of the other than it lies within the resources of pictorial skill to effect. Mirth has an undertone of gravity, and melancholy of cheerfulness. There is no antagonism between the states of mind depicted; and no rational lover, whether of contemplation or of recreation, would find any difficulty in combining the two. The limpidity of the diction is even more striking than its beauty. Never were ideas of such dignity embodied in verse so easy and familiar, and with such apparent absence of effort. The landscape-painting is that of the seventeenth century, absolutely true in broad effects, sometimes ill-defined and even inaccurate in minute details. Some of these blemishes are terrible in nineteenth-century eyes, accustomed to the photography of our Brownings and Patmores. Milton would probably have made light of them, and perhaps we owe him some thanks for thus practically refuting the heresy that inspiration implies infallibility. Yet the poetry of his blindness abounds with proof that he had made excellent use of his eyes while he had them, and no part of his poetry wants instances of subtle and delicate observation worthy of the most scrutinizing modern:--

> "Thee, chantress, oft the woods among,
> I woo, to hear thy evensong;
> And, missing thee, I walk unseen
> On the dry, smooth-shaven green."

"The song of the nightingale," remarks Peacock, "ceases about the time the grass is mown." The charm, however, is less in such detached beauties, however exquisite, than in the condensed opulence--"every epithet a text for a canto," says Macaulay--and in the general impression of "plain living and high thinking," pursued in the midst of every charm of nature and every refinement of culture, combining the ideal of Horton with the ideal of Cambridge.

"Lycidas" is far more boldly conventional, not merely in the treatment of landscape, but in the general conception and machinery. An initial effort of the imagination is required to feel with the poet; it is not wonderful that no such wing bore up the solid Johnson. Talk of Milton and his fellow-collegian as shepherds! "We know that they never drove afield, and that they had no flocks to batten." There is, in fact, according to Johnson, neither nature nor truth nor art nor pathos in the poem, for all these things are inconsistent with the introduction of a shepherd of souls in the character of a shepherd of sheep. A nineteenth-century reader, it may be hoped, finds no more difficulty in idealizing Edward King as a shepherd than in personifying the ocean calm as "sleek Panope and all her sisters," which, to be sure, may have been a trouble to Johnson. If, however, Johnson is deplorably prosaic, neither can we agree with Pattison that "in 'Lycidas' we have reached the high-water mark of English Poesy and of Milton's own production." Its innumerable beauties are rather exquisite than magnificent. It is an elegy, and cannot, therefore, rank as high as an equally consummate example of epic, lyric, or dramatic art. Even as elegy it is surpassed by the other great English masterpiece, "Adonais," in fire and grandeur. There is no incongruity in "Adonais" like the introduction of "the pilot of the Galilean lake"; its invective and indignation pour naturally out of the subject; their expression is not, as in "Lycidas," a splendid excrescence. There is no such example of sustained eloquence in "Lycidas" as the seven concluding stanzas of "Adonais" beginning, "Go thou to Rome." But the balance is redressed by the fact that the beauties of "Adonais" are the inimitable. Shelley's eloquence is even too splendid for elegy. It wants the dainty thrills and tremors of subtle versification, and the witcheries of verbal magic in which "Lycidas" is so rich--"the opening eyelids of the morn;" "smooth-sliding Mincius, crowned with vocal reeds;" Camus's garment, "inwrought with figures dim;" "the great vision of the guarded mount;" "the tender stops of various quills;" "with eager thought warbling his Doric lay." It will be noticed that these exquisite phrases have little to do with Lycidas himself, and it is a fact not to be ignored, that though Milton and Shelley doubtless felt more deeply than Dryden when he composed his scarcely inferior threnody on Anne Killegrew, whom he had never seen, both might have found subjects of grief that touched them more nearly. Shelley tells us frankly that "in another's woe he wept his own." We cannot doubt of whom Milton was thinking when he wrote:

"Fame is the spur that the clear spirit doth raise,
(That last infirmity of noble mind)
To scorn delights, and live laborious days;
But the fair guerdon when we hope to find,
And think to burst out into sudden blaze,

Comes the blind Fury with the abhorred shears,
And slits the thin-spun life. 'But not the praise,'
Phoebus replied, and touched my trembling ears;
'Fame is no plant that grows on mortal soil,
Nor in the glistering foil
Set off to the world, nor in broad rumour lies;
But lives and spreads aloft by those pure eyes,
And perfect witness of all-judging Jove;
As he pronounces lastly on each deed,
much fame in heaven expect thy meed.'"

"Comus," the richest fruit of Milton's early genius, is the epitome of the man at the age at which he wrote it. It bespeaks the scholar and idealist, whose sacred enthusiasm is in some danger of contracting a taint of pedantry for want of acquaintance with men and affairs. The Elder Brother is a prig, and his dialogues with his junior reveal the same solemn insensibility to the humorous which characterizes the kindred genius of Wordsworth, and would have provoked the kindly smile of Shakespeare. It is singular to find the inevitable flaw of "Paradise Lost" prefigured here, and the wicked enchanter made the real hero of the piece. These defects are interesting, because they represent the nature of Milton as it was then, noble and disinterested to the height of imagination, but self-assertive, unmellowed, angular. They disappear entirely when he expatiates in the regions of exalted fancy, as in the introductory discourse of the Spirit, and the invocation to Sabrina. They recur when he moralizes; and his morality is too interwoven with the texture of his piece to be other than obtrusive. He fatigues with virtue, as Lucan fatigues with liberty; in both instances the scarcely avoidable error of a young preacher. What glorious morality it is no one need be told; nor is there any poem in the language where beauties of thought, diction, and description spring up more thickly than in "Comus." No drama out of Shakespeare has furnished such a number of the noblest familiar quotations. It is, indeed, true that many of these jewels are fetched from the mines of other poets: great as Milton's obligations, to Nature were, his obligations to books were greater. But he has made all his own by the alchemy of his genius, and borrows little but to improve. The most remarkable coincidence is with a piece certainly unknown to him--Calderon's "Magico Prodigioso," which was first acted in 1637, the year of the publication of "Comus," a great year in the history of the drama, for the "Cid" appeared in it also. The similarity of the situations of Justina tempted by the Demon, and the Lady in the power of Comus, has naturally begotten a like train of thought in both poets.

"Comus. Nay, Lady, sit; if I but wave this wand,
Your nerves are all chained up in alabaster,
And you a statue, or, as Daphne was,
Root-bound, that fled Apollo.

Lady.
Fool, do not boast
Thou can'st not touch the freedom of my mind
With all thy charms, although this corporal rind
Thou hast immanacled, while Heaven sees good."

"Justina. Thought is not in my power, but action is.
I will not move my foot to follow thee.

Demon. But a far mightier wisdom than thine own
Exerts itself within thee, with such power
Compelling thee to that which it inclines
That it shall force thy step; how wilt thou then
Resist, Justina?

Justina. By my free will.

Demon.
I
Must force thy will.

Justina.

It is invincible.
It were not free if thou had'st power upon it."

It must be admitted that where the Spaniard and the Englishman come directly into competition the former excels. The dispute between the Lady and Comus may be, as Johnson says it is, "the most animating and affecting scene in the drama;" but, tried by the dramatic test which Calderon bears so well, it is below the exigencies and the possibilities of the subject. Nor does the poetry here, quite so abundantly as in the other scenes in this unrivalled "suite of speeches," atone for the deficiencies of the play.

It is a just remark of Pattison's that "in a mind of the consistent texture of Milton's, motives are secretly influential before they emerge in consciousness." In September, 1637, Milton had complained to Diodati of his cramped situation in the country, and talked of taking chambers in London. Within a few months we find this vague project matured into a settled scheme of foreign travel. One tie to home had been severed by the death of his mother in the preceding April; and his father was to find another prop of his old age in his second son, Christopher, about to marry and reside with him. "Lycidas" had appeared meanwhile, or was to appear, and its bold denunciation of the Romanizing clergy might well offend the ruling powers. The atmosphere at home was, at all events, difficult breathing for an impotent patriot; and Milton may have come to see what we so clearly see in "Comus," that his asperities and limitations needed contact with the world. Why speak of the charms of Italy, in themselves sufficient allurement to a poet and scholar? His father, trustful and unselfish as of old, found the considerable sum requisite for a prolonged foreign tour; and in April, 1638, Milton, provided with excellent introductions from Sir Henry Wootton and others, seeks the enrichment and renovation of his genius in Italy:--

"And tricks his beams, and with new-spangled ore
Flames in the forehead of the morning sky."

CHAPTER III.

Four times has a great English poet taken up his abode in "the paradise of exiles," and remained there until deeply imbued with the spirit of the land. The Italian residence of Byron and Shelley, of Landor and Browning, has infused into English literature a new element which has mingled with its inmost essence. Milton's brief visit could not be of equal moment. Italian letters had already done their utmost for him; and he did not stay long enough to master the secret of Italian life. A real enthusiasm for Italy's classical associations is indicated by his original purpose of extending his travels to Greece, an enterprise at that period requiring no little disdain of hardship and peril. But it would have been an anachronism if he could have contemplated the comprehensive and scientific scheme of self-culture by Italian influences of every kind which, a hundred and fifty years later, was conceived and executed by Goethe. At the time of Milton's visit Italian letters and arts sloped midway in their descent from the Renaissance to the hideous but humorous rococo so graphically described by Vernon Lee. Free thought had perished along with free institutions in the preceding century, and as a consequence, though the physical sciences still numbered successful cultivators, originality of mind was all but extinct. Things, nevertheless, wore a gayer aspect than of late. The very completeness of the triumph of secular and spiritual despotism had made them less suspicious, surly, and austere. Spanish power was visibly decaying. The long line of *zelanti* Popes had come to an end; and it was thought that if the bosom of the actual incumbent could be scrutinized, no little complacency in Swedish victories over the Faith's defenders would be found. An atmosphere of toleration was diffusing itself, bigotry was imperceptibly getting old-fashioned, the most illustrious victim of the Inquisition was to be well-nigh the last. If the noble and the serious could not be permitted, there was no ban upon the amiable and the frivolous: never had the land been so full of petty rhymesters, antiquarian triflers, and gregarious literati, banded to play at authorship in academies, like the seven Swabians leagued to kill the hare. For the rest, the Italy of Milton's day, its superstition and its scepticism, and the sophistry that strove to make the two as one; its monks and its bravoes; its processions and its pantomimes; its cult of the Passion and its cult of Paganism; the opulence of its past and the impotence of its present; will be found depicted by sympathetic genius in the second volume of "John Inglesant."

Milton arrived in Paris about the end of April or beginning of May. Of his short stay there it is only known that he was received with distinction by the English Ambassador, Lord Scudamore, and owed to him an introduction to one of the greatest men in Europe, Hugo Grotius, then residing at Paris as envoy from Christina of Sweden. Travelling by way of Nice, Genoa, Leghorn, and Pisa, he arrived about the beginning of August at Florence; where, probably by the aid of good recommendations, he "immediately contracted the acquaintance of many noble and learned," and doubtless found, with the author of "John Inglesant," that "nothing can be more delightful than the first few days of life in Italy in the company of polished and congenial men." The Florentine academies, he implies answered one of the purposes of modern clubs, and enabled the traveller to multiply one good introduction into many. He especially mentions Gaddi, Dati, Frescobaldi, Coltellini, Bonmattei, Chimentelli, and Francini, of all of whom a full account will be found in Masson. Two of them, Dati and Francini, have linked their names with Milton's by their encomiums on him inserted in his works. The key-note of these surprising productions is struck by Francini when he remarks that the heroes of England are accounted in Italy superhuman. If this is so, Dati may be justified in comparing a young man on his first and last foreign tour to the travelled Ulysses; and Francini in declaring that Thames rivals Helicon in virtue of Milton's Latin poems, which alone the panegyrist could read. Truly, as Smollett says, Italian is the language of compliments. If ludicrous, however, the flattery is not nauseous, for it is not wholly insincere. Amid all conventional exaggerations there is an under-note of genuine feeling, showing that the writers really had received a deep impression from Milton, deeper than they could well explain or understand. The bow drawn at a venture did not miss the mark, but it is a curious reflection that those of his performances which would really have justified their utmost enthusiasm were hieroglyphical to them. Such of his literary exercises as they could understand consisted, he says, of "some trifles which I had in memory composed at under twenty or thereabout; and other things which I had shifted, in scarcity of books and conveniences, to patch up among them." The former class of compositions may no doubt be partly identified with his college declamations and Latin verses. What the "things patched up among them" may have been is unknown. It is curious enough that his acquaintance with the Italian literati should have been the means of preserving one of their own compositions, the "Tina" of Antonio Malatesti, a series of fifty sonnets on a mistress, sent to him in manuscript by the author, with a dedication to the ***illustrissimo signore et padrone osservatissimo***. The pieces were not of a kind to be approved by the laureate of chastity, and annoyance at the implied slur upon his morals may account for his omission of Malatesti from the list of his Italian acquaintance. He carried the MS. home, nevertheless, and a copy of it, finding its way back to Italy in the eighteenth century, restored Malatesti's fifty indiscretions to the Italian Parnassus. That his intercourse with men of culture involved freedom of another sort we learn from himself. "I have sate among their learned men," he says, "and been counted happy to be born in such a place of philosophic freedom as they supposed England was, while they themselves did nothing but bemoan the servile condition into which learning amongst them was brought, that this was it which had damped the glory of Italian wits; that nothing had been written there now these many years but flattery and fustian." Italy had never acquiesced in her degradation, though for a century and a half to come she could only protest in such conventicles as those frequented by Milton.

The very type and emblem of the free spirit of Italy, crushed but not conquered, then inhabited Florence in the person of "the starry Galileo," lately released from confinement at Arcetri, and allowed to dwell in the city under such severe restraint of the Inquisition that no Protestant should have been able to gain access to him. It may not have been until Milton's second visit in March, 1639, when Galileo had returned to his villa, that the English stranger stood unseen before him. The meeting between the two great blind men of their century is one of the most picturesque in history; it would have been more pathetic still if Galileo could have known that his name would be written in "Paradise Lost," or Milton could have foreseen that within thirteen years he too would see only with the inner eye, but that the calamity which disabled the astronomer would restore inspiration to the poet. How deeply he was impressed appears, not merely from the famous comparison of Satan's shield to the moon enlarged in "the Tuscan artist's optic glass," but by the ventilation in the fourth and eighth books of "Paradise Lost," of the points at issue between Ptolemy and Copernicus:--

"Whether the sun predominant in heaven
Rise on the earth, or earth rise on the sun,
He from the east his flaming road begin,
Or she from west her silent course advance
With inoffensive pace, that spinning sleeps
On her soft axle, while she paces even,
And bears thee soft with the smooth air along."

It would be interesting to know if Milton's Florentine acquaintance included that romantic adventurer, Robert Dudley, strange prototype of Shelley in face and fortune, whom Lord Herbert of Cherbury and Dean Bargrave encountered at Florence, but whom Milton does not mention. The next stage in his pilgrimage was the Eternal City, by this time resigned to live upon its past. The revenues of which Protestant revolt had deprived it were compensated by the voluntary contributions of the lovers of antiquity and art; and it had become under Paul V. one of the centres of European finance. Recent Popes had added splendid architectural embellishments, and the tendency to secular display was well represented by Urban VIII., a great gatherer and a great dispenser of wealth, an accomplished amateur in many arts, and surrounded by a tribe of nephews, inordinately enriched by their indulgent uncle. Milton arrived early in October. The most vivid trace of his visit is his presence at a magnificent concert given by Cardinal Barberini, who, "himself waiting at the doors, and seeking me out in so great a crowd, nay, almost laying hold of me by the hand, admitted me within in a truly most honourable manner." There he heard the singer, Leonora Baroni, to whom he inscribed three Latin epigrams, omitted from the fifty-six compositions in honour of her published in the following year. But we may see her as he saw her in the frontispiece, reproduced in Ademollo's monograph upon her. The face is full of sensibility, but not handsome. She lived to be a great lady, and if any one spoke of her artist days she would say, *Chi le ricercava queste memorie?* Next to hers, the name most entwined with Milton's Roman residence is that of Lucas Holstenius, a librarian of the Vatican. Milton can have had little respect for a man who had changed his religion to become the dependant of Cardinal Barberini, but Holstenius's obliging reception of him extorted his gratitude, expressed in an eloquent letter. Of the venerable ruins and masterpieces of ancient and modern art which have inspired so many immortal compositions, Milton tells us nothing, and but one allusion to them is discoverable in his writings. The study of antiquity, as distinguished from that of classical authors, was not yet a living element in European culture: there is also truth in Coleridge's observation that music always had a greater attraction for Milton than plastic art.

After two months' stay in Rome, Milton proceeded to Naples, whence, after two months' residence, he was recalled by tidings of the impending troubles at home, just as he was about to extend his travels to Sicily and Greece. The only name associated with his at Naples is that of the Marquis Manso, then passing his seventy-ninth year with the halo of reverence due to a veteran who fifty years ago had soothed and shielded Tasso, and since had protected Marini. He now entertained Milton with equal kindness, little dreaming that in return for hospitality he was receiving immortality. Milton celebrated his desert as the friend of poets, in a Latin poem of singular elegance, praying for a like guardian of his own fame, in lines which should never be absent from the memory of his biographers. He also unfolded the project which he then cherished of an epic on King Arthur, and assured Manso that Britain was not wholly barbarous, for the Druids were really very considerable poets. He is silent on Chaucer and Shakespeare. Manso requited the eulogium with an epigram and two richly-wrought cups, and told Milton that he would have shown him more observance still if he could have abstained from religious controversy. Milton had not acted on Sir Henry Wootton's advice to him, *il volto sciolto, i pensieri stretti.* "I had made this resolution with myself," he says, "not of my own accord to introduce conversation about religion; but, if interrogated respecting the faith, whatsoever I should suffer, to dissemble nothing." To this resolution he adhered, he says, during his second two months' visit to Rome, notwithstanding threats of Jesuit molestation, which probably were not serious. At Florence his friends received him with no less warmth than if they had been his countrymen, and with them he spent another two months. His way to Venice lay through Bologna and Ferrara, and if his sonnets in the Italian language were written in Italy, and all addressed to the same person, it was probably at Bologna, since the lady is spoken of as an inhabitant of "Reno's grassy vale," and the Reno is a river between Bologna and Ferrara. But there are many difficulties in the way of this theory, and, on the whole, it seems most reasonable to conclude that the sonnets were composed in England, and that their autobiographical character is at least doubtful. That nominally inscribed to Diodati, however, would well suit Leonora Baroni. Diodati had been buried in Blackfriars on August 27, 1638, but Milton certainly did not learn the fact until after his visit to Naples, and possibly not until he came to pass some time at Geneva with Diodati's uncle. He had come to Geneva from Venice, where he had made some stay, shipping off to England a cargo of books collected in Italy, among which were many of "immortal notes and Tuscan air." These, we may assume, he found awaiting him when he again set foot on his native soil, about the end of July, 1639.

Milton's conduct on his return justifies Wordsworth's commendation:--

"Thy heart
The lowliest duties on herself did lay."

Full, as his notebooks of the period attest, of magnificent aspiration for "flights above the Aonian mount," he yet quietly sat down to educate his nephews, and lament his friend. His brother-in-law Phillips had been dead eight years, leaving two boys, Edward and John, now about nine and eight respectively. Mrs. Phillips's second marriage had added two daughters to the family, and from whatever cause, it was thought best that the education of the sons should be conducted by their uncle. So it came to pass that "he took him a lodging in St. Bride's Churchyard, at the house of one Russel, a tailor;" Christopher Milton continuing to live with his father.

We may well believe that when the first cares of resettlement were over, Milton found no more urgent duty than the bestowal of a funeral tribute upon his friend Diodati. The "Epitaphium Damonis" is the finest of his Latin poems, marvellously picturesque in expression, and inspired by true manly grief. In Diodati he had lost perhaps the only friend whom, in the most sacred sense of the term, he had ever possessed; lost him when far away and unsuspicious of the already accomplished stroke; lost him when returning to his side with aspirations to be imparted, and intellectual treasures to be shared. ***Bis ille miser qui serus amavit.*** All this is expressed with earnest emotion in truth and tenderness, surpassing "Lycidas," though void of the varied music and exquisite felicities which could not well be present in the conventionalized idiom of a modern Latin poet. The most pathetic passage is that in which he contrasts the general complacency of animals in their kind with man's dependence for sympathy on a single breast; the most biographically interesting where he speaks of his plans for an epic on the story of Arthur, which he seems about to undertake in earnest. But the impulses from without which generally directed the course of this seemingly autocratic, but really susceptible, nature, urged him in quite a different direction: for some time yet he was to live, not make a poem.

The tidings which, arriving at Naples about Christmas, 1638, prevailed upon Milton to abandon his projected visit to Sicily and Greece, were no doubt those of the revolt of Scotland, and Charles's resolution to quell it by force of arms. Ere he had yet quitted Italy, the King's impotence had been sufficiently demonstrated, and about a month ere he stood on English soil the royal army had "disbanded like the break-up of a school." Milton may possibly have regretted his hasty return, but before many months had passed it was plain that the revolution was only beginning. Charles's ineffable infatuation brought on a second Scottish war, ten times more ridiculously disastrous than the first, and its result left him no alternative but the convocation (November, 1640) of the Long Parliament, which sent Laud to the Tower and Strafford to the block, cleared away servile judges and corrupt ministers, and made the persecuted Puritans persecutors in their turn. Not a member of this grave assemblage, perhaps, but would have laughed if told that not its least memorable feat was to have prevented a young schoolmaster from writing an epic.

Milton had by this time found the lodgings in St. Bride's Churchyard insufficient for him, and had taken a house in Aldersgate Street, beyond the City wall, and suburban enough to allow him a garden. "This street," writes Howell, in 1657, "resembleth an Italian street more than any other in London, by reason of the spaciousness and uniformity of the buildings and straightness thereof, with the convenient distance of the houses." He did not at this time contemplate mixing actively in political or religious controversy.

> "I looked about to see if I could get any place that would hold
> myself and my books, and so I took a house of sufficient size in
> the city; and there with no small delight I resumed my intermitted
> studies; cheerfully leaving the event of public affairs, first to
> God, and then to those to whom the people had committed that
> task."

But this was before the convocation of the Long Parliament. When it had met,

> "Perceiving that the true way to liberty followed on from these
> beginnings, inasmuch also as I had so prepared myself from my
> youth that, above all things, I could not be ignorant what is of
> Divine and what of human right, I resolved, though I was then
> meditating certain other matters, to transfer into this struggle
> all my genius and all the strength of my industry."

Milton's note-books, to be referred to in another place, prove that he did not even then cease to meditate themes for poetry, but practically he for eighteen years ceased to be a poet.

There is no doubt something grating and unwelcome in the descent of the scholar from regions of serene culture to fierce political and religious broils. But to regret with Pattison that Milton should, at this crisis of the State, have turned aside from poetry to controversy is to regret that "Paradise Lost" should exist. Such a work could not have proceeded from one indifferent to the public weal, and if Milton had been capable of forgetting the citizen in the man of letters we may be sure that "a little grain of conscience" would ere long have "made him sour." It is sheer literary fanaticism to speak with Pattison of "the prostitution of genius to political party." Milton is as much the idealist in his prose as in his verse; and although in his pamphlets he sides entirely with one of the two great parties in the State, it is not as its instrument, but as its prophet and monitor. He himself tells us that controversy is highly repugnant to him.

"I trust to make it manifest with what small willingness I endure to interrupt the pursuit of no less hopes than these, and leave a calm and pleasing solitariness, fed with cheerful and confident thoughts, to embark in a troubled sea of noises and hoarse disputes, put from beholding the bright countenance of truth in the quiet and still air of delightful studies, to come in to the dim reflection of hollow antiquities sold by the seeming bulk."

But he felt that if he allowed such motives to prevail with him, it would be said to him:

"Timorous and ungrateful, the Church of God is now again at the foot of her insulting enemies, and thou bewailest, What matters it for thee or thy bewailing? When time was, thou would'st not find a syllable of all that thou hast read or studied to utter on her behalf. Yet ease and leisure was given thee for thy retired thoughts, but of the sweat of other men. Thou hast the diligence, the parts, the language of a man, if a vain subject were to be adorned or beautified; but when the cause of God and His Church was to be pleaded, for which purpose that tongue was given thee which thou hast, God listened if He could hear thy voice among His zealous servants, but thou wert dumb as a beast; from henceforward be that which thine own brutish silence hath made thee."

A man with "Paradise Lost" in him must needs so think and act, and, much as it would have been to have had another "Comus" or "Lycidas," were not even such well exchanged for a hymn like this, the high-water mark of English impassioned prose ere Milton's mantle fell upon Ruskin?

"Thou, therefore, that sittest in light and glory unapproachable.

Parent of angels and men! next, Thee I implore, Omnipotent King, Redeemer of that lost remnant whose nature Thou didst assume, ineffable and everlasting Love! And Thou, the third subsistence of Divine Infinitude, illuminating Spirit, the joy and solace of created things! one Tri-personal godhead! look upon this Thy poor and almost spent and expiring Church, leave her not thus a prey to these importunate wolves, that wait and think long till they devour Thy tender flock; these wild boars that have broke into Thy vineyard, and left the print of their polluting hoofs on the souls of Thy servants. O let them not bring about their damned designs that stand now at the entrance of the bottomless pit, expecting the watchword to open and let out those dreadful locusts and scorpions to reinvolve us in that pitchy cloud of infernal darkness, where we shall never more see the sun of Thy truth again, never hope for the cheerful dawn, never more hear the bird of morning sing. Be moved with pity at the afflicted state of this our shaken monarchy, that now lies labouring under her throes, and struggling against the grudges of more dreaded calamities.

"O Thou, that, after the impetuous rage of five bloody inundations, and the succeeding sword of intestine war, soaking the land in her own gore, didst pity the sad and ceaseless revolution of our swift and thick-coming sorrows; when we were quite breathless of Thy free grace didst motion peace and terms of covenant with us; and, having first well-nigh freed us from anti-Christian thraldom, didst build up this Britannic Empire to a glorious and enviable height, with all her daughter-islands about her; stay us in this felicity, let not the obstinacy of our half-obedience and will-worship bring forth that viper of sedition, that for these fourscore years hath been breeding to eat through the entrails of our peace; but let her cast her abortive spawn without the danger of this travailing and throbbing kingdom: that we may still remember in our solemn thanksgivings, how, for

us, the northern ocean, even to the frozen Thule, was scattered
with the proud shipwrecks of the Spanish Armada, and the very maw
of Hell ransacked, and made to give up her concealed destruction,
ere she could vent it in that horrible and damned blast.

"O how much more glorious will those former deliverances appear,
when we shall know them not only to have saved us from greatest
miseries past, but to have reserved us for greatest happiness to
come? Hitherto Thou hast but freed us, and that not fully, from
the unjust and tyrannous claim of Thy foes, now unite us entirely
and appropriate us to Thyself, tie us everlastingly in willing
homage to the prerogative of Thy eternal throne.

"And now we know, O Thou, our most certain hope and defence, that
Thine enemies have been consulting all the sorceries of the great
whore, and have joined their plots with that sad, intelligencing
tyrant that mischiefs the world with his mines of Ophir, and lies
thirsting to revenge his naval ruins that have larded our seas:
but let them all take counsel together, and let it come to nought;
let them decree, and do Thou cancel it; let them gather
themselves, and be scattered; let them embattle themselves, and be
broken; let them embattle, and be broken, for Thou art with us.

"Then amidst the hymns and hallelujahs of saints, some one may
perhaps be heard offering at high strains in new and lofty
measures, to sing and celebrate Thy Divine mercies and marvellous
judgments in this land throughout all ages; whereby this great and
warlike nation, instructed and inured to the fervent and continual
practice of truth and righteousness, and casting far from her the
rags of her old vices, may press on hard to that high and happy
emulation to be found the soberest, wisest, and most Christian
people at that day, when Thou, the Eternal and shortly-expected
King, shalt open the clouds to judge the several kingdoms of the

world, and distributing national honours and rewards to religious
and just commonwealths, shall put an end to all earthly tyrannies,
proclaiming Thy universal and mild monarchy through heaven and
earth; where they undoubtedly, that by their labours, counsels,
and prayers, have been earnest for the common good of religion,
and their country, shall receive above the inferior orders of the
blessed, the regal addition of principalities, legions, and
thrones into their glorious titles, and in supereminence of
beatific vision, progressing the dateless and irrevoluble circle
of eternity, shall clasp inseparable hands with joy and bliss, in
over-measure for ever.

"But they contrary, that by the impairing and diminution of the
true faith, the distresses and servitude of their country, aspire
to high dignity, rule and promotion here, after a shameful end in
this life (which God grant them), shall be thrown down eternally
into the darkest and deepest gulf of Hell, where, under the
despiteful control, the trample and spurn of all the other damned,
that in the anguish of their torture, shall have no other ease
than to exercise a raving and bestial tyranny over them as their
slaves and negroes, they shall remain in that plight for ever, the
basest, the lowermost, the most dejected, most underfoot, and
down-trodden vassals of perdition."

The five pamphlets in which Milton enunciated his views on Church Government fall into two well-marked chronological divisions. Three--"Of Reformation
touching Church Discipline in England," "Of Prelatical Episcopacy," "Animadver-
sions upon the Remonstrant's Defence against Smectymnuus"--which appeared almost simultaneously, belong to the middle of 1641, when the question of episcopacy was fiercely agitated. Two--"The Reason of Church Government urged against
Prelacy," and "The Apology for Smectymnuus,"[1] belong to the early part of 1642,
when the bishops had just been excluded from the House of Lords. To be just to
Milton we must put ourselves in his position. At the present day forms of church

government are usually debated on the ground of expediency, and even those to whom they seem important cannot regard them as they were regarded by Milton's contemporaries. Many may protest against Episcopacy receiving especial recognition from the State, but no one dreams of abolishing it, or of endowing another form of ecclesiastical administration in its room. It is no longer contended that the national religion should be changed, the contention is that no religion should be national, but that all should be placed on an impartial footing. But Milton at this time desired a theocracy, and nothing doubted that he could produce a pattern agreeable in every respect to the Divine will if only Prelacy could be hurled after Popery. The controversy, therefore, assumed far grander proportions than would be possible in our day, when it is three-fourths a protest against the airs of superiority which the alleged successors of the Apostles think it becoming to assume towards teachers whose education and circumstances approach more closely than their own to the Apostolic model. What would seem exaggerated now was then perfectly in place. Milton, in his own estimation, had a theme for which the cloven tongues of Pentecost were none too fiery, or the tongues of angels too melodious. As bursts of impassioned prose-poetry the finest passages in these writings have never been surpassed, nor ever will be equalled so long as short sentences prevail, and the interminable period must not unfold itself in heights and hollows like the incoming tide of ocean, nor peal forth melodious thunder like a mighty organ. But, considered as argumentative compositions, they are exceedingly weak. No masculine head could be affected by them; but a manly heart may easily imbibe the generous contagion of their noble enthusiastic idealism. No man with a single fibre of ideality or enthusiasm can help confessing that Milton has risen to a transcendent height, and he may imagine that it has been attained by the ladder of reason rather than the pinion of poetry. Such an one may easily find reasons for agreeing with Milton in many inspired outbursts of eloquence simulating the logic that is in fact lacking to them. The following splendid passage, for instance, and there are very many like it, merely proves that a seat in the House of Lords is not essential to the episcopal office, which no one ever denied. It would have considerable force if the question involved the nineteenth century one of the Pope's temporal sovereignty:--

"Certainly there is no employment more honourable, more worthy to take up a great spirit, more requiring a generous and free nurture, than to be the messenger and herald of heavenly truth from God to man, and by the faithful work of holy doctrine to procreate a number of faithful men, making a kind of creation like to God's by infusing his spirit and likeness into them, to their salvation, as God did into him; arising to what climate soever he turn him, like that Sun of Righteousness that sent him, with healing in his wings, and new light to break in upon the chill and gloomy hearts of his hearers, raising out of darksome barrenness a delicious and fragrant spring of saving knowledge and good works. Can a man thus employed find himself discontented or dishonoured for want of admittance to have a pragmatical voice at sessions and jail deliveries? or because he may not as a judge sit out the wrangling noise of litigious courts to shrive the purses of unconfessing and unmortified sinners, and not their souls, or be discouraged though men call him not lord, whereas the due performance of his office would gain him, even from lords and princes, the voluntary title of father?"

When it was said of Robespierre, ***cet homme ira bien loin, car il croit tout ce qu'il dit***, it was probably meant that he would attain the chief place in the State. It might have been said of Milton in the literal sense. The idealist was about to apply his principles of church polity to family life, to the horror of many nominal allies. His treatise on Divorce was the next of his publications in chronological order, but is so entwined with his domestic life that it will be best to postpone it until we again take up the thread of his personal history, and to pass on for the present to his next considerable writings, his tracts on education and on the freedom of the press.

Milton's tract on Education, like so many of his performances, was the fruit of an impulse from without. "Though it be one of the greatest and noblest designs that can be thought on, and for want of which this nation perishes, I had not at this time been induced but by your earnest entreaties and serious conjurements." The efficient cause thus referred to existed in the person of Samuel Hartlib, philanthropist and polypragmatist, precursor of the Franklins and Rumfords of the succeeding century.

The son of a Polish exile of German extraction, Hartlib had settled in England about 1627. He found the country behindhand both economically and socially, and with benign fervour applied himself to its regeneration. Agriculture was his principal hobby, and he effected much towards its improvement in England, rather however by editing the unpublished treatises of Weston and Child than by any direct contributions of his own. Next among the undertakings to which he devoted himself were two of no less moment than the union of British and foreign Protestants, and the reform of English education by the introduction of the methods of Comenius. This Moravian pastor, the Pestalozzi of his age, had first of men grasped the idea that the ordinary school methods were better adapted to instil a knowledge of words than a knowledge of things. He was, in a word, the inventor of object lessons. He also strove to organize education as a connected whole from the infant school to the last touch of polish from foreign travel. Milton alludes almost scornfully to Comenius in his preface to Hartlib, but his tract is nevertheless imbued with the Moravian's principles. His aim, like Comenius's, is to provide for the instruction of all, "before the years of puberty, in all things belonging to the present and future life." His view is as strictly utilitarian as Comenius's. "Language is but the instrument conveying to us things useful to be known." Of the study of language as intellectual discipline he says nothing, and his whole course of instruction is governed by the desire of imparting useful knowledge. Whatever we may think of the system of teaching which in our day allows a youth to leave school disgracefully ignorant of physical and political geography, of history and foreign languages, it cannot be denied that Milton goes into the opposite extreme, and would overload the young mind with more information than it could possibly digest. His scheme is further vitiated by a fault which we should not have looked for in him, indiscriminate reverence for the classical writers, extending to subjects in which they were but children compared with the moderns. It moves something more than a smile to find ingenuous youth referred to Pliny and Solinus for instruction in physical science; and one wonders what the agricultural Hartlib thought of the proposed course of "Cato, Varro, and Columella," whose precepts are adapted for the climate of Italy. Another error, obvious to any dunce, was concealed from Milton by his own intellectual greatness. He legislates for a college of Miltons. He never suspects that the course he is prescribing would be beyond the abilities of nine hundred and ninety-nine scholars in a thousand, and that the thousandth would die of it. If a difficulty occurs he contemptuously puts it aside. He has not provided for Italian, but can it not "be easily learned at any odd hour"? "Ere this time the Hebrew tongue" (of which we have not hitherto heard a syllable), "might have been gained, whereto it would be no impossibility to add the Chaldee and the Syrian dialect." This sublime confidence in the resources of the human intellect is grand, but it marks out Milton as an idealist, whose mission it was rather to animate mankind by the greatness of his thoughts than to devise practical schemes for human improvement. As an ode or poem on education, Milton's tract, doubtless, has delivered many a teacher and scholar from bondage to routine; and no man's aims are so high or his thoughts so generous that he might not be further profited and stimulated by reading it. As a practical treatise it is only valuable for its emphatic denunciation of the folly of teasing youth, whose element is the concrete, with grammatical abstractions, and the advice to proceed to translation as soon as possible, and to keep it up steadily throughout the whole course. Neglect of this precept is the principal reason why so many youths not wanting in capacity, and assiduously taught, leave school with hardly any knowledge of languages. Milton's scheme is also remarkable for its bold dealing with day schools and universities, which it would have entirely superseded.

The next publication of Milton's is another instance of the dependence of his intellectual workings upon the course of events outside him. We owe the "Areopagitica," not to the lonely overflowings of his soul, or even to the disinterested observation of public affairs, but to the real jeopardy he had incurred by his neglect to get his books licensed. The Long Parliament had found itself, in 1643, with respect to the Press, very much in the position of Lord Canning's government in India at the time of the Mutiny. It marks the progress of public opinion that, whereas the Indian Government only ventured to take power to prevent inopportune publication with many apologies, and as a temporary measure, the Parliament assumed it as self-evident that "forged, scandalous, seditious, libellous, and unlicensed papers, pamphlets, and books" had no right to exist, and should be nipped in the bud by the appointment of licensers. Twelve London ministers, therefore, were nominated to license books in divinity, which was equivalent to enacting that nothing contrary to Presbyterian orthodoxy should be published in England.[2] Other departments, not forgetting poetry and fiction, were similarly provided for. The ordinance is dated June 14, 1643. Milton had always contemned the licensing regulations previously existing, and within a month his brain was busy with speculations which no reverend licenser could have been expected to confirm with an imprimatur. About August 1st the "Doctrine and Discipline of Divorce" appeared, with no recognition of or from a licenser; and the second edition, published in the following February, equally infringed the Parliamentary ordinance. No notice appears to have been taken until the election of a new Master of the Stationers' Company, about the middle of 1644. The Company had an interest in the enforcement of the ordinance, which was aimed at piracy as well as sedition and heresy; and whether for this reason, or at the instigation of Milton's adversaries, they (August 24th) petitioned Parliament to call him to account. The matter was referred to a committee, but more urgent business thrust it out of sight. Milton, nevertheless, had received his marching orders, and on November 24, 1644, appeared "Areopagitica; a Speech for the Liberty of Unlicensed Printing": itself unlicensed.

The "Areopagitica" is by far the best known of Milton's prose writings, being the only one whose topic is not obsolete. It is also composed with more care and art than the others. Elsewhere he seeks to overwhelm, but here to persuade. He could without insincerity profess veneration for the Lords and Commons to whom his discourse is addressed, and he spares no pains to give them a favourable opinion both of his dutifulness and his reasonableness. More than anywhere else he affects the character of a practical man, pressing home arguments addressed to the understanding rather than to the pure reason. He points out sensibly, and for him calmly, that the censorship is a Papal invention, contrary to the precedents of antiquity; that while it cannot prevent the circulation of bad books, it is a grievous hindrance to good ones; that it destroys the sense of independence and responsibility essential to a manly and fruitful literature. We hear less than might have been expected about first principles, of the sacredness of conscience, of the obligation on every man to manifest the truth as it is within him. He does not dispute that the magistrate may suppress opinions esteemed dangerous to society after they have been published; what he maintains is that publication must not be prevented by a board of licensers. He strikes at the censor, not at the Attorney-General. This judicious caution cramped Milton's eloquence; for while the "Areopagitica" is the best example he has given us of his ability as an advocate, the diction is less magnificent than usual.

Yet nothing penned by him in prose is better known than the passage beginning, "Methinks I see in my mind a noble and puissant nation;" and none of his writings contain so many seminal sentences, pithy embodiments of vital truths. "Revolutions of ages do not oft recover the loss of a rejected truth." "A dram of well-doing should be preferred before many times as much the forcible hindrance of evil doing. For God more esteems the growth and completing of one virtuous person than the restraint of ten vicious." "Opinion in good men is but knowledge in the making." "A man maybe a heretic in the truth." Towards the end the argument takes a wider sweep, and Milton, again the poet and the seer, hails with exultation the approach of the time he thinks he discerns when all the Lord's people shall be prophets. "Behold now this vast city, a city of refuge, the mansion house of liberty, encompassed and surrounded with His protection; the shop of war hath not there more anvils and hammers working to fashion out the plates and instruments of armed justice in defence of beleaguered truth, than there be pens and heads there, sitting by their studious lamps, musing, searching, revolving new notions and ideas wherewith to present, as with their homage and their fealty, the approaching reformation." He clearly indicates that he regards the licensing ordinance as not really the offspring of an honest though mistaken concern for religion and morality, but as a device of Presbyterianism to restrain this outpouring of the spirit and silence Independents as well as Royalists. Presbyterianism had indeed been weighed in the balance and found wanting, and Milton's pamphlet was the handwriting on the wall. The fine gold must have become very dim ere a Puritan pen could bring itself to indite that scathing satire on the "factor to whose care and credit the wealthy man may commit the whole managing of his religious affairs; some divine of note and estimation that must be. To him he adheres; resigns the whole warehouse of his religion, with all the locks and keys into his custody; and, indeed, makes the very person of that man his religion--esteems his associating with him a sufficient evidence and commendation of his own piety. So that a man may say his religion is now no more within himself, but is become a dividual movable, and goes and comes near him according as that good man frequents the house. He entertains him, gives him gifts, feasts him, lodges him, his religion comes home at night, prays, is liberally supped and sumptuously laid to sleep, rises, is saluted; and after the malmsey or some well-spiced brewage, and better breakfasted than He whose morning appetite would have gladly fed on green figs between Bethany and Jerusalem, his religion walks abroad at eight, and leaves his kind entertainer in the shop, trading all day without his religion." This is a startling passage. We should have pronounced hitherto that Milton's one hopeless, congenital, irremediable want, alike in literature and in life, was humour. And now, surely as ever Saul was among the prophets, behold Milton among the wits.

CHAPTER IV.

Ranging with Milton's spirit over the "fresh woods and pastures new," fore-shadowed in the closing verse of "Lycidas," we have left his mortal part in its suburban dwelling in Aldersgate Street, which he seems to have first inhabited shortly before the convocation of the Long Parliament in November, 1640. His visible occupations are study and the instruction of his nephews; by and by he becomes involved in the revolutionary tempest that rages around; and, while living like a pedagogue, is writing like a prophet. He is none the less cherishing lofty projects for epic and drama; and we also learn from Phillips that his society included "some young sparks," and may assume that he then, as afterwards--

"Disapproved that care, though wise in show,
That with superfluous burden loads the day,
And, when God sends a cheerful hour, refrains."

There is eloquent testimony of his interest in public affairs in his subscription of four pounds, a large sum in those days, for the relief of the homeless Protestants of Ulster. The progress of events must have filled him with exultation, and when at length civil war broke out in September, 1642, Parliament had no more zealous champion. His zeal, however, did not carry him into the ranks, for which some biographers blame him. But if he thought that he could serve his cause better with a pamphlet than with a musket, surely he had good reason for what he thought. It should seem, moreover, that if Milton detested the enemy's principles, he respected his pikes and guns:--

WHEN THE ASSAULT WAS INTENDED TO THE CITY
[NOVEMBER, 1642.]

Captain, or Colonel, or Knight in arms,
Whose chance on these defenceless doors may seize,
If deed of honour did thee ever please,
Guard them, and him within protect from harms.
He can requite thee, for he knows the charms
That call fame on such gentle acts as these,
And he can spread thy name o'er lands and seas,
Whatever clime the sun's bright circle warms.
Lift not thy spear against the Muse's bower:
The great Emathian conqueror bid spare
The house of Pindarus, when temple and tower
Went to the ground; and the repeated air
Of sad Electra's poet had the power
To save the Athenian walls from ruin bare.

If this strain seems deficient in the fierceness befitting a besieged patriot, let it be remembered that Milton's doors were literally defenceless, being outside the rampart of the City.

We now approach the most curious episode of Milton's life, and the most irreconcilable with the conventional opinion of him. Up to this time this heroic existence must have seemed dull to many, for it has been a life without love. He has indeed, in his beautiful Sonnet to the Nightingale (about 1632), professed himself a follower of Love: but if so, he has hitherto followed at a most respectful distance. Yet he had not erred, when in the Italian sonnet, so finely rendered in Professor Masson's biography, he declared the heart his vulnerable point:--

"Young, gentle-natured, and a simple wooer,
Since from myself I stand in doubt to fly,
Lady, to thee my heart's poor gift would I

Offer devoutly; and by tokens sure
I know it faithful, fearless, constant, pure,
In its conceptions graceful, good, and high.
When the world roars, and flames the startled sky;
In its own adamant it rests secure;
As free from chance and malice ever found,
And fears and hopes that vulgar minds confuse,
As it is loyal to each manly thing
And to the sounding lyre and to the Muse.
Only in that part is it not so sound
Where Love hath set in it his cureless sting."

It is highly probable that the very reaction from party strife turned the young man's fancies to thoughts of love in the spring of 1643. Escorted, we must fear, by a chorus of mocking cuckoos, Milton, about May 21st, rode into the country on a mysterious errand. It is a ghoulish and ogreish idea, but it really seems as if the elder Milton quartered his progeny upon his debtors, as the ichneumon fly quarters hers upon caterpillars. Milton had, at all events for the last sixteen years, been regularly drawing interest from an Oxfordshire squire, Richard Powell of Forest Hill, who owed him L500, which must have been originally advanced by the elder Milton. The Civil War had no doubt interfered with Mr. Powell's ability to pay interest, but, on the other hand, must have equally impaired Milton's ability to exact it; for the Powells were Cavaliers, and the Parliament's writ would run but lamely in loyal Oxfordshire. Whether Milton went down on this eventful Whitsuntide in the capacity of a creditor cannot now be known; and a like uncertainty envelops the precise manner of the metamorphosis of Mary Powell into Mary Milton. The maiden of seventeen may have charmed him by her contrast to the damsels of the metropolis, she may have shielded him from some peril, such as might easily beset him within five miles of the Royalist headquarters, she may have won his heart while pleading for her harassed father; he may have fancied hers a mind he could mould to perfect symmetry and deck with every accomplishment, as the Gods fashioned and decorated Pandora. Milton also seems to imply that his, or his bride's, better judgment was partly overcome by "the persuasion of friends, that acquaintance, as it increases, will amend all." It is possible, too, that he had long been intimate with his debtor's family, and that Mary had previously made an impression upon him. If not, his was the most preposterously precipitate of poets' marriages; for a month after leaving home he presented a mistress to his astounded nephews and house-keeper. The newly-wedded pair were accompanied or quickly followed by a bevy of the bride's friends and relatives, who danced and sang and feasted for a week in the quiet Puritan house, then departed--and after a few weeks Milton finds himself moved to compose his tract on the "Doctrine and Discipline of Divorce."

How many weeks? The story seemed a straightforward one until Professor Masson remarked what had before escaped attention. According to Phillips, an inmate of the house at the period--"By that time she had for a month, or thereabouts, led a philosophical life (after having been used to a great house, and much company and joviality), her friends, possibly incited by her own desire, made earnest suit by letter to have her company the remaining part of the summer, which was granted, on condition of her return at the time appointed, Michaelmas or thereabout. Michaelmas being come, and no news of his wife's return, he sent for her by letter, and receiving no answer sent several other letters, which were also unanswered, so that at last he dispatched down a foot-messenger; but the messenger came back without an answer. He thought it would be dishonourable ever to receive her again after such a repulse, and accordingly wrote two treatises," &c. Here we are distinctly assured that Mary Milton's desertion of her husband, about Michaelmas, was the occasion of his treatise on divorce. It follows that Milton's tract must have been written after Michaelmas. But the copy in the British Museum belonged to the bookseller Thomason, who always inscribed the date of publication on every tract in his collection, when it was known to him, and his date, as Professor Masson discovered, is August 1. Must we believe that Phillips's account is a misrepresentation? Must we, in Pattison's words, "suppose that Milton was occupying himself with a vehement and impassioned argument in favour of divorce for incompatibility of temper, during the honeymoon"? It would certainly seem so, and if Milton is to be vindicated it can only be by attention to traits in his character, invisible on its surface, but plainly discoverable in his actions.

The grandeur of Milton's poetry, and the dignity and austerity of his private life, naturally incline us to regard him as a man of iron will, living by rule and reason, and exempt from the sway of passionate impulse. The incident of his marriage, and not this incident alone, refutes this conception of his character; his nature was as lyrical and mobile as a poet's should be. We have seen "Comus" and "Lycidas" arise at another's bidding, we shall see a casual remark beget "Paradise Regained." He never attempts to utter his deepest religious convictions until caught by the contagious enthusiasm of a revolution. If any incident in his life could ever have compelled him to speak or die it must have been the humiliating issue of his matrimonial adventure. To be cast off after a month's trial like an unsatisfactory servant, to forfeit the hope of sympathy and companionship which had allured him into the married state, to forfeit it, unless the law could be altered, for ever! The feelings of any sensitive man must find some sort of expression in such an emergency. At another period what Milton learned in suffering would no doubt have been taught in song. But pamphlets were then the order of the day, and Milton's "Doctrine and Discipline of Divorce," in its first edition, is as much the outpouring of an overburdened heart as any poem could have been. It bears every mark of a hasty composition, such as may well have been written and printed within the last days of July, following Mary Milton's departure. It is short. It deals with the most obvious aspects of the question. It is meagre in references and citations; two authors only are somewhat vaguely alleged, Grotius and Beza. It does not contain the least allusion to his domestic circumstances, nor anything unless the thesis itself, that could hinder his wife's return. Everything betokens that it was composed in the bitterness of wounded feeling upon the incompatibility becoming manifest; but that he had not yet arrived at the point of demanding the application of his general principle to his own special case. That point would be reached when Mary Milton deliberately refused to return, and the chronology of the greatly enlarged second edition, published in the following February, entirely confirms Phillips's account. In one point only he must be wrong. Mary Milton's return to her father's house cannot have been a voluntary concession on Milton's part, but must have been wrung from him after bitter contentions. Could we look into the household during those weeks of wretchedness, we should probably find Milton exceedingly deficient in consideration for the inexperienced girl of half his age, brought from a gay circle of friends and kindred to a grave, studious house. But it could not well have been otherwise. Milton was constitutionally unfit "to soothe and fondle," and his theories cannot have contributed to correct his practice. His "He for God only, she for God in him," condenses every fallacy about woman's true relation to her husband and her Maker. In his Tractate on Education there is not a word on the education of girls, and yet he wanted an intellectual female companion. Where should the woman be found at once submissive enough and learned enough to meet such inconsistent exigencies? It might have been said to him as afterwards to Byron: "You talk like a Rosicrucian, who will love nothing but a sylph, who does not believe in the existence of a sylph, and who yet quarrels with the whole universe for not containing a sylph."

If Milton's first tract on divorce had not been a mere impromptu, extorted by the misery of finding "an image of earth and phlegm" in her "with whom he looked to be the co-partner of a sweet and gladsome society," he would certainly have rendered his argument more cogent and elaborate. The tract, in its inspired portions, is a fine impassioned poem, fitter for the Parliament of Love than the Parliament at Westminster. The second edition is far more satisfactory as regards that class of arguments which alone were likely to impress the men of his generation, those derived from the authority of the Scriptures and of divines. In one of his principal points all Protestants and philosophers will confess him to be right, his reference of the matter to Scripture and reason, and repudiation of the mediaeval canon law. It is not here, nevertheless, that Milton is most at home. The strength of his position is his lofty idealism, his magnificent conception of the institution he discusses, and his disdain for whatever degrades it to conventionality or mere expediency. "His ideal of true and perfect marriage," says Mr. Ernest Myers, "appeared to him so sacred that he could not admit that considerations of expediency might justify the law in maintaining sacred any meaner kind, or at least any kind in which the vital element of spiritual harmony was not." Here he is impregnable and above criticism, but his handling of the more sublunary departments of the subject must be unsatisfactory to legislators, who have usually deemed his sublime idealism fitter for the societies of the blest than for the imperfect communities of mankind. When his "doctrine and discipline" shall have been sanctioned by lawgivers, we may be sure that the world is already much better, or much worse.

As the girl-wife vanishes from Milton's household her place is taken by the venerable figure of his father. The aged man had removed with his son Christopher to Reading, probably before August, 1641, when the birth of a child of his name-

-Christopher's offspring as it should seem--appears in the Reading register. Chris-topher was to exemplify the law of reversion to a primitive type. Though not yet a Roman Catholic like his grandfather, he had retrograded into Royalism, without becoming on that account estranged from his elder brother. The surrender of Read-ing to the Parliamentary forces in April, 1643, involved his "dissettlement," and the migration of his father to the house of John, with whom he was moreover better in accord in religion and politics. Little external change resulted, "the old gentleman," says Phillips, "being wholly retired to his rest and devotion, with the least trouble imaginable." About the same time the household received other additions in the shape of pupils, admitted, Phillips is careful to assure us, by way of favour, as M. Jourdain selected stuffs for his friends. Milton's pamphlet was perhaps not yet pub-lished, or not generally known to be his, or his friends were indifferent to public sentiment. Opinion was unquestionably against Milton, nor can he have profited much by the support, however practical, of a certain Mrs. Attaway, who thought that "she, for her part, would look more into it, for she had an unsanctified husband, that did not walk in the way of Sion, nor speak the language of Canaan," and by and by actually did what Milton only talked of doing. We have already seen that he had incurred danger of prosecution from the Stationers' Company, and in July, 1644, he was denounced by name from the pulpit by a divine of much note, Herbert Palmer, author of a book long attributed to Bacon. But, if criticised, he was read. By 1645 his Divorce tract was in the third edition, and he had added three more pamphlets--one to prove that the revered Martin Bucer had agreed with him; two, the "Tet-rachordon" and "Colasterion," directed against his principal opponents, Palmer, Featley, Caryl, Prynne, and an anonymous pamphleteer, who seems to have been a somewhat contemptible person, a serving-man turned attorney, but whose pro-duction contains some not unwelcome hints on the personal aspects of Milton's controversy. "We believe you count no woman to due conversation accessible, as to you, except she can speak Hebrew, Greek, Latin, and French, and dispute against the canon law as well as you." Milton's later tracts are not specially interesting, ex-cept for the reiteration of his fine and bold idealism on the institution of marriage, qualified only by his no less strenuous insistance on the subjection of woman. He allows, however, that "it is no small glory to man that a creature so like him should be made subject to him," and that "particular exceptions may have place, if she exceed her husband in prudence and dexterity, and he contentedly yield; for then a superior and more natural law comes in, that the wiser should govern the less wise, whether male or female."

Milton's seminary, meanwhile, was prospering to such a degree as to compel him to take a more commodious house. Was it necessity or enthusiasm that kept him to a task so little compatible with the repose he must have needed even for such intellectual exercise as the "Areopagitica," much more for the high designs he had not ceased to meditate in verse? Enthusiasm, one would certainly say, only that it is impossible to tell to what extent his father's income, chiefly derived from money out at interest, may have been impaired by the confusion of the times. Whether he had done rightly or wrongly in taking the duties of a preceptor upon himself, his nephew's account attests the self-sacrificing zeal with which he discharged them: we groan as we read of hours which should have been devoted to lonely musing or noble composition passed in "increasing as it were by proxy" his knowledge of "Frontinus his Stratagems, with the two egregious poets Lucretius and Manilius." He might also have been better employed than in dictating "A tractate he thought fit to collect from the ablest of divines who have written on that subject of atheism, Amesius, Wollebius," &c. Here should be comfort for those who fear with Pattison that Milton's addiction to politics deprived us of unnumbered "Comuses." The excerpter of Amesius and Wollebius, as we have so often insisted, needed great stimulus for great achievements. Such stimulus would probably have come superabundantly if he could at this time have had his way, for the most moral of men was bent on assuming a direct antagonism to conventional morality. He had maintained that marriage ought to be dissolved for mere incompatibility; his case must have seemed much stronger now that incompatibility had produced desertion. He was not the man to shrink from acting on his opinion when the fit season seemed to him to have arrived; and in the summer of 1645 he was openly paying his addresses to "a very handsome and witty gentlewoman, one of Dr. Davis's daughters." Considering the consequences to the female partner to the contract, it is clear that Miss Davis could not be expected to entertain Milton's proposals unless her affection for him was very strong indeed. It is equally clear that he cannot be acquitted of selfishness in urging his suit unless he was quite sure of this, and his own heart also was deeply interested. An event was about to occur which seems to prove that these conditions were wanting.

Nearly two years have passed since we have heard of Mary Milton, who has been living with her parents in Oxfordshire. Her position as a nominal wife must have been most uncomfortable, but there is no indication of any effort on her part to alter it, until the Civil War was virtually terminated by the Battle of Naseby, June, 1645. Obstinate malignants had then nothing to expect but fine and forfeiture, and their son-in-law's Puritanism may have presented itself to the Powells in the light of a merciful dispensation. Rumours of Milton's suit to Miss Davis may also have reached them; and they would know that an illegal tie would be as fatal to all hopes of reconciliation as a legal one. So, one day in July or August, 1645, Milton, paying his usual call on a kinsman named Blackborough,[3] not otherwise mentioned in his life, who lived in St. Martin's-le-Grand Lane, where the General Post Office now stands, "was surprised to see one whom he thought to have never seen more, making submission and begging pardon on her knees before him." There are two similar scenes in his writings, of which this may have formed the groundwork, Dalila's visit to her betrayed husband in "Samson Agonistes," and Eve's repentance in the tenth book of "Paradise Lost." Samson replies, "Out, out, hyaena!" Eve's "lowly plight"

"in Adam wrought
Commiseration;...
As one disarmed, his anger all he lost,
And thus with peaceful words upraised her soon."

Phillips appears to intimate that the penitent's reception began like Dalila's and ended like Eve's. "He might probably at first make some show of aversion and rejection; but partly his own generous nature, more inclinable to reconciliation than to perseverance in anger and revenge, and partly the strong intercession of friends on both sides, soon brought him to an act of oblivion, and a firm league of peace for the future." With a man of his magnanimous temper, conscious no doubt that he had himself been far from blameless, such a result was to be expected. But it was certainly well that he had made no deeper impression than he seems to have done upon "the handsome and witty gentlewoman." One would like to know whether she and Mistress Milton ever met, and what they said to and thought of each other.

For the present, Mary Milton dwelt with Christopher's mother-in-law, and about September joined her husband in the more commodious house in the Barbican whither he was migrating at the time of the reconciliation. It stood till 1864, when it was destroyed by a railway company.

Soon after removing to the Barbican, Milton set his Muse's house in order, by publishing such poems, English and Latin, as he deemed worthy of presentation. It is a remarkable proof both of his habitual cunctativeness and his dependence on the suggestions of others, that he should so long have allowed such pieces to remain uncollected, and should only have collected them at all at the solicitation of the publisher, Humphrey Moseley. The transaction is most honourable to the latter. "It is not any private respect of gain," he affirms; "for the slightest pamphlet is nowadays more vendible than the works of learnedest men, but it is the love I bear to our own language.... I know not thy palate, how it relishes such dainties, nor how harmonious thy soul is: perhaps more trivial airs may please better.... Let the event guide itself which way it will, I shall deserve of the age by bringing forth into the light as true a birth as the Muses have brought forth since our famous Spenser wrote." The volume was published on Jan. 2, 1646. It is divided into two parts, with separate title-pages, the first containing the English poems, the second the Latin. They were probably sold separately. The frontispiece, engraved by Marshall, is unfortunately a sour and silly countenance, passing as Milton's, but against which he protests in four lines of Greek appended, which the worthy Marshall seems to have engraved without understanding them. The British Museum copy in the King's Library contains an additional MS. poem of considerable merit, in a hand which some have thought like Milton's, but few now believe it to have been either written or transcribed by him. It is dated 1647, but for which circumstance one might indulge the fancy that the copy had been a gift from him to some Italian friend, for the binding is Italian, and the book must have seen Italy.

Milton was now to learn what he afterwards taught, that "they also serve who only stand and wait." He had challenged obloquy in vindication of what he deemed right: the cross actually laid upon him was to fill his house with inimical and uncongenial dependants on his bounty and protection. The overthrow of the Royalist cause was utterly ruinous to the Powells. All went to wreck on the surrender of Oxford in June, 1646. The family estate was only saved from sequestration by a friendly neighbour taking possession of it under cover of his rights as creditor; the family mansion was occupied by the Parliamentarians, and the household stuff sold to the harpies that followed in their train; the "malignant's" timber went to rebuild the good town of Banbury. It was impossible for the Powells to remain in Oxford-shire, and Milton opened his doors to them as freely as though there had never been any estrangement. Father, mother, several sons and daughters came to dwell in a house already full of pupils, with what inconvenience from want of room and disquiet from clashing opinions may be conjectured. "Those whom the mere neces-sity of neighbourhood, or something else of a useless kind," he says to Dati, "has closely conjoined with me, whether by accident or the tie of law, they are the per-sons who sit daily in my company, weary me, nay, by heaven, almost plague me to death whenever they are jointly in the humour for it." Milton's readiness to receive the mother, deemed the chief instigator of her daughter's "frowardness," may have been partly due to the situation of the latter, who gave him a daughter on July 29, 1646. In January, 1647, Mr. Powell died, leaving his affairs in dire confusion. Two months afterwards Milton's father followed him at the age of eighty-four, partly cognisant, we will hope, of the gift he had bestowed on his country in his son. It was probably owing to the consequent improvement in Milton's circumstances that he about this time gave up his pupils, except his nephews, and removed to a smaller house in High Holborn, not since identified; the Powells also removing to another dwelling. "No one," he says of himself at this period, "ever saw me going about, no one ever saw me asking anything among my friends, or stationed at the doors of the Court with a petitioner's face. I kept myself almost entirely at home, managing on my own resources, though in this civil tumult they were often in great part kept from me, and contriving, though burdened with taxes in the main rather oppressive, to lead my frugal life." The traces of his literary activity at this time are few--preparations for a history of England, published long afterwards, an ode, a sonnet, correspondence with Dati, some not very successful versions of the Psalms. He seems to have been partly engaged in preparing the treatise on Chris-tian Doctrine, which was fortunately reserved for a serener day. In undertaking it at this period he was missing a great opportunity. He might have been the apostle of toleration in England, as Roger Williams had been in America. The moment was most favourable. Presbyterianism had got itself established, but could not pretend to represent the majority of the nation. It had been branded by Milton himself in the memorable line: "New Presbyter is but old Priest writ large." The Independents were for toleration, the Episcopalians had been for the time humbled by adversity, the best minds in the nation, including Cromwell, were Seekers or Latitude men, or sceptics. Here was invitation enough for a work as much greater than the "Areopagitica" as the principle of freedom of thought is greater than the most august particular application of it. Milton might have added the better half of Locke's fame to his own, and compelled the French philosophers to sit at the feet of a Bible-loving Englishman. But unfortunately no external impulse stirred him to action, as in the case of the "Areopagitica." Presbyterians growled at him occasionally; they did not fine or imprison him, or put him out of the synagogue. Thus his pen slumbered, and we are in danger of forgetting that he was, in the ordinary sense of that much-abused term, no Puritan, but a most free and independent thinker, the vast sweep of whose thought happened to coincide for a while with the narrow orbit of so-called Puritanism.

Impulse to work of another sort was at hand. On January 30, 1649, Charles the First's head rolled on the scaffold. On February 13th was published a pamphlet from Milton's hand, which cannot have been begun before the King's trial, another proof of his feverish impetuosity when possessed by an overmastering idea. The title propounds two theses with very different titles to acceptance. "The Tenure of Kings and Magistrates proving that it is lawful, and hath been held so through all ages, for any who have the power to call to account a tyrant or wicked king, and after due conviction to depose and put him to death: if the ordinary magistrate have neglected or denied to do it." That kings have no more immunity than others from the consequences of evil doing is a proposition which seemed monstrous to many in Milton's day, but which will command general assent in ours. But to lay it down that "any who has the power" may interpose to correct what he chooses to consider the laches of the lawful magistrate is to hand over the administration of the law to Judge Lynch--rather too high a price to pay for the satisfaction of bringing even a bad king to the block. Milton's sneer at "vulgar and irrational men, contesting for privileges, customs, forms, and that old entanglement of iniquity, their gibberish laws," is equivalent to an admission that his party had put itself beyond the pale of the law. The only defence would be to show that it had acted under great and overwhelming necessity; but this he takes for granted, though knowing well that it was denied by more than half the nation. His argument, therefore, is inconclusive, except that portion of it which modern opinion allows to pass without argument. He seems indeed to admit in his "Defensio Secunda" that the tract was written less to vindicate the King's execution than to saddle the protesting Presbyterians with a share of the responsibility. The diction, though robust and spirited, is not his best, and, on the whole, the most admirable feature in his pamphlet is his courage in writing it. He was to speak yet again on this theme as the mouthpiece of the Commonwealth, thus earning honour and reward; it was well to have shown first that he did not need this incentive to expose himself to Royalist vengeance, but had prompting enough in the intensity of his private convictions.

He had flung himself into a perilous breach. "Eikon Basilike"--most timely of manifestoes--had been published only four days before the appearance of "The Tenure of Kings and Magistrates." Between its literary seduction and the horror generally excited by the King's execution, the tide of public opinion was turning fast. Milton no doubt felt that no claim upon him could be equal to that which the State had a right to prefer. He accepted the office of "Secretary for Foreign Tongues" to the Committee of Foreign Affairs, a delegation from the Council of State of forty-one members, by which the country was at that time governed. Vane, Whitelocke, and Marten were among the members of the committee. The specified duties of the post were the preparation and translation of despatches from and to foreign governments. These were always in Latin,--the Council, says that sturdy Briton, Edward Phillips, "scorning to carry on their affairs in the wheedling, lisping jargon of the cringing French." But it must have been understood that Milton's pen would also be at the service of the Government outside the narrow range of official correspondence. The salary was handsome for the time--L288, equivalent to about L900 of our money. It was an honourable post, on the manner of whose discharge the credit of England abroad somewhat depended; the foreign chanceries were full of accomplished Latinists, and when Blake's cannon was not to be the mouthpiece, the Commonwealth's message needed a silver trumpet. It was also as likely as any employment to make a scholar a statesman. If in some respects it opposed new obstacles to the fulfilment of Milton's aspirations as a poet, he might still feel that it would help him to the experience which he had declared to be essential: "He who would not be frustrate of his hope to write well hereafter in laudable things, ought himself to be a true poem, that is, a composition and pattern of the best and honourablest things, not presuming to sing high praises of heroic men or famous cities, unless he have within himself the experience and the practice of all that which is praiseworthy." Up to this time Milton's experience of public affairs had been slight; he does not seem to have enjoyed the intimate acquaintance of any man then active in the making of history. In our day he would probably have entered Parliament, but that was impossible under a dispensation which allowed a Parliament to sit till a Protector turned it out of doors. He was, therefore, only acting upon his own theory, and he seems to us to have been acting wisely as well as courageously, when he consented to become a humble but necessary wheel of the machinery of administration, the Orpheus among the Argonauts of the Commonwealth.

CHAPTER V.

Milton was appointed Secretary for Foreign Tongues on March 15, 1649. He removed from High Holborn to Spring Gardens to be near the scene of his labours, and was soon afterwards provided with an official residence in Whitehall Palace, a huge intricacy of passages and chambers, of which but a fragment now remains. His first performance was in some measure a false start; for the epistle offering amity to the Senate of Hamburg, clothed in his best Latin, was so unamiably regarded by that body that the English envoy never formally delivered it. An epistle to the Dutch on the murder of the Commonwealth's ambassador, Dorislaus, by refugee Cavaliers, had a better reception; and Milton was soon engaged in drafting, not merely translating, a State paper designed for the press--observations on the peace concluded by Ormond, the Royalist commander in Ireland, with the confederated Catholics in that country, and on the protest against the execution of Charles I. volunteered by the Presbytery of Belfast. The commentary was published in May, along with the documents. It is a spirited manifesto, cogent in enforcing the necessity of the campaign about to be undertaken by Cromwell. Ireland had at the moment exactly as many factions as provinces; and never, perhaps, since the days of Strongbow had been in a state of such utter confusion. Employed in work like this, Milton did not cease to be "an eagle towering in his pride of place," but he may seem to have degenerated into the "mousing owl" when he pounced upon newswriters and ferreted unlicensed pamphlets for sedition. True, there was nothing in this occupation formally inconsistent with anything he had written in the "Areopagitica"; yet one wishes that the Council of State had provided otherwise for this particular department of the public service. Nothing but a sense of duty can have reconciled him to a task so invidious; and there is some evidence of what might well have been believed without evidence--

that he mitigated the severity of the censorship as far as in him lay. He was not to want for better occupation, for the Council of State was about to devolve upon him the charge of answering the great Royalist manifesto, "Eikon Basilike."

The controversy respecting the authorship of the "Eikon Basilike" is a remarkable instance of the degree in which literary judgment may be biassed by political prepossession. In the absence of other testimony one might almost stamp a writer as Royalist or Parliamentarian according as his verdict inclined to Charles I. or Bishop Gauden. In fact, it is no easy matter to balance the respective claims of two entirely different kinds of testimony. The external evidence of Charles's authorship is worth nothing. It is almost confined to the assertions, forty years after the publication, of a few aged Cavaliers, who were all morally certain that Charles wrote the book, and to whom a fiction supplying the accidental lack of external testimony would have seemed laudable and pious. The only wonder is that such legends are not far more numerous. On the other hand, the internal evidence seems at first sight to make for the king. The style is not dissimilar to that of the reputed royal author; the sentiments are such as would have well become him; the assumed character is supported throughout with consistency; and there are none of the slips which a fabricator might have been thought hardly able to avoid. The supposed personator of the King was unquestionably an unprincipled time-server. Is it not an axiom that a worthy book can only proceed from a worthy mind?

> "If this fail,
> The pillared firmament is rottenness,
> And earth's base built on stubble!"

Against such considerations we have to set the stubborn facts that Bishop Gauden did actually claim the authorship that he preferred his claim to the very persons who had the strongest interest in exploding it; that he invoked the testimony of those who must have known the truth, and could most easily have crushed the lie; that he convinced not only Clarendon, but Charles's own children, and received a substantial reward. In the face of these undeniable facts, the numerous circumstances used with skill and ingenuity by Dr. Wordsworth to invalidate his claim, are of little weight. The stronger the apparent objections, the more certain that the proofs in Gauden's hands must have been overwhelming, and the greater the presumption that he was merely urging what had always been known to several persons about the late king. When, with this conviction, we recur to the "Eikon," and examine it in connection with Gauden's acknowledged writings, the internal testimony against him no longer seems so absolutely conclusive. Gauden's style is by no means so bad as Hume represents it. Many remarkable parallels between it and the diction of the "Eikon" have been pointed out by Todd, and the most searching modern investigator, Doble. We may also discover one marked intellectual resemblance. Nothing is more characteristic in the "Eikon" than its indirectness. The writer is full of qualifications, limitations, allowances; he fences and guards himself, and seems always on the point of taking back what he has said, but never does; and veers and tacks, tacks and veers, until he has worked himself into port. The like peculiarity is very observable in Gauden, especially in his once-popular "Companion to the Altar." There is also a strong internal argument against Charles's authorship in the preponderance of the theological element. That this should occupy an important place in the writings of a martyr for the Church of England was certainly to be expected, but the theology of the "Eikon" has an unmistakably professional flavour. Let any man read it with an unbiassed mind, and then say whether he has been listening to a king or to a chaplain. "One of *us*," pithily comments Archbishop Herring. "I write rather like a divine than a prince," the assumed author acknowledges, or is made to acknowledge. When to these considerations is added that any scrap of the "Eikon" in the King's handwriting would have been treasured as an inestimable relic, and that no scrap was ever produced, there can be little question as to the verdict of criticism. For all practical purposes, nevertheless, the "Eikon" in Milton's time was the King's book, for everybody thought it so. Milton hints some vague suspicions, but refrains from impugning it seriously, and indeed the defenders of its authenticity will be quite justified in asserting that if Gauden had been dumb, Criticism would have been blind.

According to Selden's biographer, Cromwell was at first anxious that the "Eikon" should be answered by that consummate jurist, and it was only on his declining the task that it came into Milton's hands. That he also would have declined it but for his official position may be inferred from his own words: "I take it on me as a work assigned, rather than by me chosen or affected." His distaste may further be gauged by his tardiness; while "The Tenure of Kings and Magistrates" had been written in little more than a week, his "Eikonoklastes," a reply to a book published in February, did not appear until October 6th. His reluctance may be partly explained by his feeling that "to descant on the misfortunes of a person fallen from so high a dignity, who hath also paid his final debt both to nature and his faults, is neither of itself a thing commendable, nor the intention of this discourse." The intention it may not have been, but it was necessarily the performance. The scheme of the "Eikon" required the respondent to take up the case article by article, a thing impossible to be done without abundant "descant" of the kind which Milton deprecates. He is compelled to fight the adversary on the latter's chosen ground, and the eloquence which might have swept all before it in a discussion of general principles is frittered away in tiresome wrangling over a multitude of minutiae. His vigorous blows avail but little against the impalpable ideal with which he is contending; his arguments might frequently convince a court of justice, but could do nothing to dispel the sorcery which enthralled the popular imagination. Milton's "Eikonoklastes" had only three editions, including a translation, within the year; the "Eikon Basilike" is said to have had fifty.

Milton's reputation as a political controversialist, however, was not to rest upon "Eikonoklastes," or to be determined by a merely English public. The Royalists had felt the necessity of appealing to the general verdict of Europe, and had entrusted their cause to the most eminent classical scholar of the age. To us the idea of commissioning a political manifesto from a philologist seems eccentric; but erudition and the erudite were never so highly prized as in the seventeenth century. Men's minds were still enchained by authority, and the precedents of Agis, or Brutus, or Nehemiah, weighed like dicta of Solomon or Justinian. The man of Greek, or Latin, or Hebrew learning was, therefore, a person of much greater consequence than he is now, and so much the more if he enjoyed a high reputation and wrote good Latin. All these qualifications were combined in Claudius Salmasius, a Frenchman, who had laid scholars under an eternal obligation by his discovery of the Palatine MS. of the Anthology at Heidelberg, and who, having embraced Protestantism from conviction, lived in splendid style at Leyden, where the mere light of his countenance--for he did not teach--was valued by the University at three thousand livres a year. It seems marvellous that a man should become dictator of the republic of letters by editing "Solinus" and "The Augustan History," however ably; but an achievement like this, not a "Paradise Lost" or a "Werther" was the *sic itur ad astra* of the time. On the strength of such Salmasius had pronounced *ex cathedra* on a multiplicity of topics, from episcopacy to hair-powder, and there was no bishop and no perfumer between the Black Sea and the Irish who would not rather have the scholar for him than against him. A man, too, to be named with respect; no mere annotator, but a most sagacious critic; peevish, it might be, but had he not seven grievous disorders at once? One who had shown such independence and integrity in various transactions of his life, that we may be very sure that Charles II.'s hundred Jacobuses, if ever given or even promised, were the very least of the inducements that called him into the field against the executioners of Charles I.

Whether, however, the hundred Jacobuses were forthcoming or not, Salmasius's undertaking was none the less a commission from Charles II., and the circumstance put him into a false position, and increased the difficulty of his task. Human feeling is not easily reconciled to the execution of a bad magistrate, unless he has also been a bad man. Charles I. was by no means a bad man, only a mistaken one. He had been guilty of many usurpations and much perfidy: but he had honestly believed his usurpations within the limits of his prerogative; and his breaches of faith were committed against insurgents whom he regarded as seamen look upon pirates, or shepherds upon wolves. Salmasius, however, pleading by commission from Charles's son, can urge no such mitigating plea. He is compelled to maintain the inviolability even of wicked sovereigns, and spends two-thirds of his treatise in supporting a proposition to state which is to refute it in the nineteenth century. In the latter part he is on stronger ground. Charles had unquestionably been tried and condemned by a tribunal destitute of legal authority, and executed contrary to the wish and will of the great majority of his subjects. But this was a theme for an Englishman to handle. Salmasius cannot think himself into it, nor had he sufficient imagination to be inspired by Charles as Burke (who, nevertheless, has borrowed from him) was to be inspired by Marie Antoinette.

His book--entitled "Defensio Regia pro Carolo I."--appeared in October or November, 1649. On January 8, 1650, it was ordered by the Council of State "that Mr. Milton do prepare something in answer to the Book of Salmasius, and when he hath done it bring it to the Council." There were many reasons why he should be entrusted with this commission, and only one why he should not; but one which would have seemed conclusive to most men. His sight had long been failing. He had already lost the use of one eye, and was warned that if he imposed this additional strain upon his sight, that of the other would follow. He had seen the greatest astronomer of the age condemned to inactivity and helplessness, and could measure his own by the misery of Galileo. He calmly accepted his duty along with its penalty, without complaint or reluctance. If he could have performed his task in the spirit with which he undertook it, he would have produced a work more sublime than "Paradise Lost."

This, of course, was not possible. The efficiency of a controversialist in the seventeenth century was almost estimated in the ratio of his scurrility, especially when he wrote Latin. From this point of view Milton had got his opponent at a tremendous disadvantage. With the best will in the world, Salmasius had come short in personal abuse, for, as the initiator of the dispute, he had no personal antagonist. In denouncing the general herd of regicides and parricides he had hurt nobody in particular, while concentrating all Milton's lightnings on his own unlucky head. They seared and scathed a literary dictator whom jealous enemies had long sighed to behold insulted and humiliated, while surprise equalled delight at seeing the blow dealt from a quarter so utterly unexpected. There is no comparison between the invective of Milton and of Salmasius; not so much from Milton's superiority as a controversialist, though this is very evident, as because he writes under the inspiration of a true passion. His scorn of the presumptuous intermeddler who has dared to libel the people of England is ten thousand times more real than Salmasius's official indignation at the execution of Charles. His contempt for Salmasius's pedantry is quite genuine; and he revels in ecstasies of savage glee when taunting the apologist of tyranny with his own notorious subjection to a tyrannical wife. But the reviler in Milton is too far ahead of the reasoner. He seems to set more store by his personalities than by his principles. On the question of the legality of Charles's execution he has indeed little argument to offer; and his views on the wider question of the general responsibility of kings, sound and noble in themselves, suffer from the mass of irrelevant quotation with which it was in that age necessary to prop them up. The great success of his reply ("Pro Populo Anglicano Defensio") arose mainly from the general satisfaction that Salmasius should at length have met with his match.

The book, published in or about March, 1651, instantly won over European public opinion, so far as the question was a literary one. Every distinguished foreigner then resident in London, Milton says, either called upon him to congratulate him, or took the opportunity of a casual meeting. By May, says Heinsius, five editions were printed or printing in Holland, and two translations. "I had expected nothing of such quality from the Englishman," writes Vossius. The Diet of Ratisbon ordered "that all the books of Miltonius should be searched for and confiscated." Parisian magistrates burned it on their own responsibility. Salmasius himself was then at Stockholm, where Queen Christina, who did not, like Catherine II., recognize the necessity of "standing by her order," could not help letting him see that she regarded Milton as the victor. Vexation, some thought, contributed as much as climate to determine his return to Holland. He died in September, 1653, at Spa, as, remote from books, but making his memory his library, he was penning his answer. This unfinished production, edited by his son, appeared after the Restoration, when the very embers of the controversy had grown cold, and the palm of literary victory had been irrevocably adjudged to Milton.

Milton could hear the plaudits, he could not see the wreaths. The total loss of his sight may be dated from March, 1652, a year after the publication of his reply. It was then necessary to provide him with an assistant--that no change should have been made in his position or salary shows either the value attached to his services or the feeling that special consideration was due to one who had voluntarily given his eyes for his country. "The choice lay before me," he writes, "between dereliction of a supreme duty and loss of eyesight; in such a case I could not listen to the physician, not if AEsculapius himself had spoken from his sanctuary; I could not but obey that inward monitor, I know not what, that spoke to me from heaven." In September, 1654, he described the symptoms of his infirmity to his friend, the Greek Philaras, who had flattered him with hopes of cure from the dexterity of the French oculist Thevenot. He tells him how his sight began to fail about ten years before; how in the morning he felt his eyes shrinking from the effort to read anything; how the light of a candle appeared like a spectrum of various colours; how, little by little, darkness crept over the left eye; and objects beheld by the right seemed to waver to and fro; how this was accompanied by a kind of dizziness and heaviness which weighed upon him throughout the afternoon. "Yet the darkness which is perpetually before me seems always nearer to a whitish than to a blackish, and such that, when the eye rolls itself, there is admitted, as through a small chink, a certain little trifle of light." Elsewhere he says that his eyes are not disfigured:

"Clear
To outward view of blemish or of spot."

These symptoms have been pronounced to resemble those of glaucoma. Milton himself, in "Paradise Lost," hesitates between amaurosis ("drop serene") and cataract ("suffusion"). Nothing is said of his having been recommended to use glasses or other precautionary contrivances. Cheselden was not yet, and the oculist's art was probably not well understood. The sufferer himself, while not repining or despairing of medical assistance, evidently has little hope from it. "Whatever ray of hope may be for me from your famous physician, all the same, as in a case quite incurable, I prepare and compose myself accordingly. My darkness hitherto, by the singular kindness of God, amid rest and studies, and the voices and greetings of friends, has been much easier to bear than that deathly one. But if, as is written, 'Man doth not live by bread alone, but by every word that proceedeth out of the mouth of God,' what should prevent me from resting in the belief that eyesight lies not in eyes alone, but enough for all purposes in God's leading and providence? Verily, while only He looks out for me, and provides for me, as He doth; teaching me and leading me forth with His hand through my whole life, I shall willingly, since it hath seemed good to Him, have given my eyes their long holiday. And to you I now bid farewell, with a mind not less brave and steadfast than if I were Lynceus himself for keenness of sight." Religion and philosophy, of which no brighter example was ever given, did not, in this sore trial, disdain the support of a manly pride:--

"What supports me, dost thou ask?
The conscience, friend, to have lost them overplied
In liberty's defence, my noble task,
O! which all Europe rings from side to side;
This thought might lead me through the world's vain mask,
Content though blind, had I no better guide."

Noble words, and Milton might well triumph in his victory in the field of intellectual combat. But if his pamphlet could have put Charles the First's head on again, then, and then only, could it have been of real political service to his party.

Milton's loss of sight was accompanied by domestic sorrow, though perhaps not felt with special acuteness. Since the birth of his eldest daughter in 1646, his wife had given him three more children--a daughter, born in October, 1648; a son, born in March, 1650, who died shortly afterwards; and another daughter, born in May, 1652. The birth of this child may have been connected with the death of the mother in the same or the following month. The household had apparently been peaceful, but it is unlikely that Mary Milton can have been a companion to her husband, or sympathized with such fraction of his mind as it was given her to understand. She must have become considerably emancipated from the creeds of her girlhood if his later writings could have been anything but detestable to her; and, on the whole, much as one pities her probably wasted life, her disappearance from the scene, if tragic in her ignorance to the last of the destiny that might have been hers, is not unaccompanied with a sense of relief. Great, nevertheless, must have been the blind poet's embarrassment as the father of three little daughters. Much evil, it is to be feared, had already been sown; and his temperament, his affliction, and his circumstances alike nurtured the evil yet to come. He was then living in Petty France, Westminster, having been obliged, either by the necessities of his health or of the public service, to give up his apartments in Whitehall. The house stood till 1877, a forlorn tenement in these latter years; far different, probably, when the neighbourhood was fashionable and the back windows looked on St. James's Park. It is associated with other celebrated names, having been owned by Bentham and occupied by Hazlitt.

The controversy with Salmasius had an epilogue, chiefly memorable in so far as it occasioned Milton to indulge in autobiography, and to record his estimate of some of the heroes of the Commonwealth. Among various replies to his "Defensio," not deserving of notice here, appeared one of especial acrimony, "Regii Sanguinis Clamor ad Coelum," published about August, 1652. It was a prodigy of scurrilous invective, bettering the bad example which Milton had set (but which hundreds in that age had set him) of ridiculing Salmasius's foibles when he should have been answering his arguments. Having been in Italy, he was taxed with Italian vices: he would have been accused of cannibalism had his path lain towards the Caribee Islands. A fulsome dedication to Salmasius tended to fix the suspicion of authorship upon Alexander Morus, a Frenchman of Scotch extraction, Professor of Sacred History at Amsterdam, and pastor of the Walloon Church, then an inmate of Salmasius's house, who actually had written the dedication and corrected the proof. The real author, however, was Peter Du Moulin, ex-rector of Wheldrake, in Yorkshire. The dedicatory ink was hardly dry ere Morus was involved in a desperate quarrel with Salmasius through the latter's imperious wife, who accused Morus of having been over-attentive to her English waiting-maid, whose patronymic is lost to history under the Latinized form of Bontia. Failing to make Morus marry the damsel, she sought to deprive him of his ecclesiastical and professorial dignities. The correspondence of Heinsius and Vossius shows what intense amusement the affair occasioned to such among the scholars of the period as were unkindly affected towards Salmasius. Morus was ultimately acquitted, but his position in Holland had become uncomfortable, and he was glad to accept an invitation from the congregation at Charenton, celebrated for its lunatics. Understanding, meanwhile, that Milton was preparing a reply, and being naturally unwilling to brave invective in the cause of a book which he had not written, and of a patron who had cast him off, he protested his innocence of the authorship, and sought to ward off the coming storm by every means short of disclosing the writer. Milton, however, esteeming his Latin of much more importance than Morus's character, and justly considering with Voltaire, "que cet Habacuc etait capable de tout," persisted in exhibiting himself as the blind Cyclop dealing blows amiss. His reply appeared in May, 1654, and a rejoinder by Morus produced a final retort in August, 1655. Both are full of personalities, including a spirited description of the scratching of Morus's face by the injured Bontia. These may sink into oblivion, while we may be grateful for the occasion which led Milton to express himself with such fortitude and dignity on his affliction and its alleviations:--"Let the calumniators of God's judgments cease to revile me, and to forge their superstitious dreams about me. Let them be assured that I neither regret my lot nor am ashamed of it, that I remain unmoved and fixed in my opinion, that I neither believe nor feel myself an object of God's anger, but actually experience and acknowledge His fatherly mercy and kindness to me in all matters of greatest moment--especially in that I am able, through His consolation and His strengthening of my spirit, to acquiesce in His divine will, thinking oftener of what He has bestowed upon me than of what He has withheld: finally, that I would not exchange the consciousness of what I have done with that of any deed of theirs, however righteous, or part with my always pleasant and tranquil recollection of the same." He adds that his friends cherish him, study his wants, favour him with their society more assiduously even than before, and that the Commonwealth treats him with as much honour as if, according to the customs of the Athenians of old, it had decreed him public support for his life in the Prytaneum.

Milton's tract is also interesting for its pen-portraits of some of the worthies of the Commonwealth, and its indications of his own views on the politics of his troubled times. Bradshaw is eulogized with great elegance and equal truth for his manly courage and strict consistency. "Always equal to himself, and like a consul re-elected for another year, so that you would say he not only judged the King from his tribunal, but is judging him all his life." This was matter of notoriety: one may hope that Milton had equal reason for his praise of Bradshaw's affability, munificence, and placability. The comparison of Fairfax to the elder Scipio Africanus is more accurate than is always or often the case with historical parallels, and by a dexterous turn, surprising if we have forgotten the scholar in the controversialist, Fairfax's failure in statesmanship, as Milton deemed it, is not only extenuated, but is made to usher in the more commanding personality of Cromwell. Caesar, says Johnson, had not more elegant flattery than Cromwell received from Milton: nor Augustus, he might have added, encomiums more heartfelt and sincere. Milton was one of the innumerable proofs that a man may be very much of a Republican without being anything of a Liberal. He was as firm a believer in right divine as any Cavalier, save that in his view such right was vested in the worthiest; that is, practically, the strongest. An admirable doctrine for 1653,--how unfit for 1660 remained to be discovered by him. Under its influence he had successively swallowed Pride's Purge, the execution of Charles I. by a self-constituted tribunal, and Cromwell's expulsion of the scanty remnant of what had once seemed the more than Roman senate of 1641. There is great reason to believe with Professor Masson that a tract vindicating this violence was actually taken down from his lips. It is impossible to say that he was wrong. Cromwell really was standing between England and anarchy. But Milton might have been expected to manifest some compunction at the disappointment of his own brilliant hopes, and some alarm at the condition of the vessel of the State reduced to her last plank. Authority actually had come into the hands of the kingliest man in England, valiant and prudent, magnanimous and merciful. But Cromwell's life was precarious, and what after Cromwell? Was the ancient constitution, with its halo of antiquity, its settled methods, and its substantial safeguards, wisely exchanged for one life, already the mark for a thousand bullets? Milton did not reflect, or he kept his reflections to himself. The one point on which he does seem nervous is lest his hero should call himself what he is. The name of Protector even is a stumbling-block, though one *can* get over it. "You have, by assuming a title likest that of Father of your Country, allowed yourself to be, one cannot say elevated, but rather brought down so many stages from your real sublimity, and as it were forced into rank for the public convenience." But there must be no question of a higher title:--

"You have, in your far higher majesty, scorned the title of King.
And surely with justice: for if in your present greatness you were
to be taken with that name which you were able when a private man
to reduce and bring to nothing, it would be almost as if, when by
the help of the true God you had subdued some idolatrous nation,
you were to worship the gods you had yourself overcome."

This warning, occurring in the midst of a magnificent panegyric, sufficiently vindicates Milton against the charge of servile flattery. The frank advice which he gives Cromwell on questions of policy is less conclusive evidence: for, except on the point of disestablishment, it was such as Cromwell had already given himself. Professor Masson's excellent summary of it may be further condensed thus--1. Reliance on a council of well-selected associates. 2. Absolute voluntaryism in religion. 3. Legislation not to be meddlesome or over-puritanical. 4. University and scholastic endowments to be made the rewards of approved merit. 5. Entire liberty of publication at the risk of the publisher. 6. Constant inclination towards the generous view of things. The advice of an enthusiastic idealist, Puritan by the accident of his times, but whose true affinities were with Mill and Shelley and Rousseau.

An interesting question arises in connection with Milton's official duties: had he any real influence on the counsels of Government? or was he a mere secretary? It would be pleasing to conceive of him as Vizier to the only Englishman of the day whose greatness can be compared with his; to imagine him playing Aristotle to Cromwell's Alexander. We have seen him freely tendering Cromwell what might have been unpalatable advice, and learn from Du Moulin's lampoon that he was accused of having behaved to the Protector with something of dictatorial rudeness. But it seems impossible to point to any direct influence of his mind in the administration; and his own department of Foreign Affairs was neither one which he was peculiarly qualified to direct, nor one in which he was likely to differ from the ruling powers. "A spirited foreign policy" was then the motto of all the leading men of England. Before Milton's loss of sight his duties included attendance upon foreign envoys on State occasions, of which he must afterwards have been to a considerable extent relieved. The collection of his official correspondence published in 1676 is less remarkable for the quantity of work than the quality. The letters are not very numerous, but are mostly written on occasions requiring a choice dignity of expression. "The uniformly Miltonic style of the greater letters," says Professor Masson, "utterly precludes the idea that Milton was only the translator of drafts furnished him." We seem to see him sitting down to dictate, weighing out the fine gold of his Latin sentences to the stately accompaniment, it may be, of his chamber-organ. War is declared against the Dutch; the Spanish ambassador is reproved for his protraction of business; the Grand Duke of Tuscany is warmly thanked for protecting English ships in the harbour of Leghorn; the French king is admonished to indemnify English merchants for wrongful seizure; the Protestant Swiss cantons are encouraged to fight for their religion; the King of Sweden is felicitated on the birth of a son and heir, and on the Treaty of Roeskilde; the King of Portugal is pressed to use more diligence in investigating the attempted assassination of the English minister; an ambassador is accredited to Russia; Mazarin is congratulated on the capture of Dunkirk. Of all his letters, none can have stirred Milton's personal feelings so deeply as the epistle of remonstrance to the Duke of Savoy on the atrocious massacre of the Vaudois Protestants (1655); but the document is dignified and measured in tone. His emotion found relief in his greatest sonnet; blending, as Wordsworth implies, trumpet notes with his habitual organ-music; the most memorable example in our language of the fire and passion which may inspire a poetical form which some have deemed only fit to celebrate a "mistress's eyebrow"[4]:--

"Avenge, O Lord, Thy slaughtered saints, whose bones
Lie scattered on the Alpine mountains cold;
Even them who kept Thy truth so pure of old,
When all our fathers worshipped stocks and stones.
Forget not: in Thy book record their groans
Who were Thy sheep, and in their ancient fold
Slain by the bloody Piemontese that rolled
Mother with infant down the rocks. Their moans
The vales redoubled to the hills, and they
To Heaven. Their martyred blood and ashes sow
O'er all the Italian fields, where still doth sway
The triple tyrant; that from these may grow
A hundredfold, who, having learned Thy way,
Early may fly the Babylonian woe."

This is what Johnson calls "carving heads upon cherry-stones!"

Milton's calamity had, of course, required special assistance. He had first had Weckherlin as coadjutor, then Philip Meadows, finally Andrew Marvell. His emoluments had been reduced, in April, 1655, from L288 to L150 a year, but the diminished allowance was made perpetual instead of annual, and seems to have been intended as a retiring pension. He nevertheless continued to work, drawing salary at the rate of L200 a year, and his pen was never more active than during the last months of Oliver's Protectorate. He continued to serve under Richard, writing eleven letters between September, 1658, and February, 1659. With two letters for the restored Parliament after Richard's abdication, written in May, 1659, Milton, though his formal supersession was yet to come, virtually bade adieu to the Civil Service:--

"God doth not need
Either man's work, or his own gifts; who best
Bear His mild yoke, they serve Him best: His state

Is kingly; thousands at His bidding speed,
And post o'er land and ocean without rest;
They also serve who only stand and wait."

The principal domestic events in Milton's life, meanwhile, had been his marriage with Katherine, daughter of an unidentified Captain Woodcock, in November, 1656; and the successive loss of her and an infant daughter in February and March, 1658. It is probable that Milton literally never saw his wife, whose worth and the consequent happiness of the fifteen months of their too brief union, are sufficiently attested by his sonnet on the dream in which he fancied her restored to him, with the striking conclusion, "Day brought back my night." Of his daughters at the time, much may be conjectured, but nothing is known; his nephews, whose education had cost him such anxious care, though not undutiful in their personal relations with him, were sources of uneasiness from their own misadventures, and might have been even more so as sinister omens of the ways in which the rising generation was to walk. The fruits of their bringing up upon the egregious Lucretius and Manilius were apparently "Satyr against Hypocrites," *i.e.*, Puritans; "Mysteries of Love and Eloquence;" "Sportive Wit or Muses' Merriment," which last brought the Council down upon John Phillips as a propagator of immorality. In his nephews Milton might have seen, though we may be sure he did not see, how fatally the austerity of the Commonwealth had alienated those who would soon determine whether the Commonwealth should exist. Unconscious of the "engine at the door," he could spend happy social hours with attached friends--Andrew Marvell, his assistant in the secretaryship and poetical satellite; his old pupil Cyriack Skinner; Lady Ranelagh; Oldenburg, the Bremen envoy, destined to fame as Secretary of the Royal Society and the correspondent of Spinoza; and a choice band of "enthusiastic young men who accounted it a privilege to read to him, or act as his amanuenses, or hear him talk." A sonnet inscribed to one of these, Henry Lawrence, gives a pleasing picture of the British Homer in his Horatian hour:--

"Lawrence, of virtuous father virtuous son,
Now that the fields are dank, and ways are mire,
Where shall we sometimes meet, and by the fire

Help waste a sullen day, what may be won
From the hard season gaining? Time will run
On smoother, till Favonius re-inspire
The frozen earth, and clothe in fresh attire
The lily and rose, that neither sowed nor spun.
What neat repast shall feast us, light and choice,
Of Attic taste, with wine, whence we may rise
To hear the lute well touched, or artful voice
Warble immortal notes and Tuscan air?
He who of those delights can judge, and spare
To interpose them oft, is not unwise."

CHAPTER VI.

"Thought by thought in heaven-defying minds
As flake by flake is piled, till some great truth
Is loosened, and the nations echo round."

These lines, slightly altered from Shelley, are more applicable to the slow growth and sudden apparition of "Paradise Lost" than to most of those births of genius whose maturity has required a long gestation. In most such instances the work, however obstructed, has not seemed asleep. In Milton's case the germ slumbered in the soil seventeen or eighteen years before the appearance of a blade, save one of the minutest. After two or three years he ceased, so far as external indications evince, to consciously occupy himself with the idea of "Paradise Lost." His country might well claim the best part of his energies, but even the intervals of literary leisure were given to Amesius and Wollebius rather than Thamyris and Maeonides. Yet the material of his immortal poem must have gone on accumulating, or inspiration, when it came at last, could not so soon have been transmuted into song. It can hardly be doubted that his cruel affliction was, in truth, the crowning blessing of his life. Remanded thus to solemn meditation, he would gradually rise to the height of his great argument; he would reflect with alarm how little, in comparison with his powers, he had yet done to "sustain the expectation he had not refused:" and he would come little by little to the point when he could unfold his wings upon his own impulse, instead of needing, as always hitherto, the impulse of others. We cannot tell what influence finally launched this high-piled avalanche of thrice-sifted snow. The time is better ascertained. Aubrey refers it to 1658, the last year of Oliver's Protectorate. As Cromwell's death virtually closed Milton's official labours, a Genie, overshadowing land and sea, arose from the shattered vase of the Latin Secretaryship.

Nothing is more interesting than to observe the first gropings of genius in pursuit of its aim. Ample insight, as regards Milton, is afforded by the precious manuscripts given to Trinity College, Cambridge, by Sir Henry Newton Puckering (we know not how he got them), and preserved by the pious care of Charles Mason and Sir Thomas Clarke. By the portion of the MSS. relating to Milton's drafts of projected poems, which date about 1640-1642, we see that the form of his work was to have been dramatic, and that, in respect of subject, the swift mind was divided between Scripture and British History. No fewer than ninety-nine possible themes--sixty-one Scriptural, and thirty-eight historical or legendary--are jotted down by him. Four of these relate to "Paradise Lost." Among the most remarkable of the other subjects are "Sodom" (the plan is detailed at considerable length, and, though evidently impracticable, is interesting as a counterpart of "Comus"), "Samson Marrying," "Ahab," "John the Baptist," "Christus Patiens," "Vortigern," "Alfred the Great," "Harold," "Athirco" (a very striking subject from a Scotch legend), and "Macbeth," where Duncan's ghost was to have appeared instead of Banquo's, and seemingly taken a share in the action. "Arthur," so much in his mind when he wrote the "Epitaphium Damonis," does not appear at all. Two of the drafts of "Paradise Lost" are mere lists of *dramatis personae*, but the others indicate the shape which the conception had then assumed in Milton's mind as the nucleus of a religious drama on the pattern of the mediaeval mystery or miracle play. Could he have had any vague knowledge of the autos of Calderon? In the second and more complete draft Gabriel speaks the prologue. Lucifer bemoans his fall and altercates with the Chorus of Angels. Eve's temptation apparently takes place off the stage, an arrangement which Milton would probably have reconsidered. The plan would have given scope for much splendid poetry, especially where, before Adam's expulsion, "the Angel causes to pass before his eyes a masque of all the evils of this life and world," a conception traceable in the eleventh book of "Paradise Lost." But it is grievously cramped in comparison with the freedom of the epic, as Milton must soon have discovered. That he worked upon it appears from the extremely interesting fact, preserved by Phillips, that Satan's address to the Sun is part of a dramatic speech which, according to Milton's plan in 1642 or 1643, would have formed the exordium of his tragedy. Of the literary sources which may have originated or enriched the conception of "Paradise Lost" in Milton's mind we shall speak hereafter. It must suffice for the present to remark that his purpose had from the first been didactic. This is particularly visible in the notes of alternative subjects in his manuscripts, many of which palpably allude to the ecclesiastical and political incidents of his time, while one is strikingly prophetic of his own defence of the execution of Charles I. "The contention between the father of Zimri and Eleazar whether he ought to have slain his son without law; next the ambassadors of the Moabites expostulating about Cosbi, a stranger and a noblewoman, slain by Phineas. It may be argued about reformation and punishment illegal, and, as it were, by tumult. After all arguments driven home, then the word of the Lord may be brought, acquitting and approving Phineas." It was his earnest aim at all events to compose something "doctrinal and exemplary to a nation." "Whatsoever," he says in 1641, "whatsoever in religion is holy and sublime, in virtue amiable or grave, whatsoever hath passion or admiration in all the changes of that which is called fortune from without, or the wily subtleties and refluxes of man's thoughts from within--all these things with a solid and treatable smoothness to paint out and describe; teaching over the whole book of sanctity and virtue, through all the instances of example, with much delight, to those especially of soft and delicious temper who will not so much as look upon Truth herself unless they see her elegantly drest, that, whereas the paths of honesty and good life appear more rugged and difficult, though they be indeed easy and pleasant, they would then appear to all men easy and pleasant though they were rugged and difficult in deed." An easier task than that of "justifying the ways of God to man" by the cosmogony and anthropology of "Paradise Lost."

If it is true--and the fact seems well attested--that Milton's poetical vein flowed only from the autumnal equinox to the vernal[5], he cannot well have commenced "Paradise Lost" before the death of Cromwell, or have made very great progress with it ere his conception of his duty called him away to questions of ecclesiastical policy. The one point on which he had irreconcilably differed from Cromwell was that of a State Church; Cromwell, the practical man, perceiving its necessity, and Milton, the idealist, seeing only its want of logic. Unfortunately, this inconsequence existed only for the few thinkers who could in that age rise to the acceptance of Milton's premises. In his "Treatise of Civil Power in Ecclesiastical Causes," published in February, 1659, he emphatically insists that the civil magistrate has neither the right nor the power to interfere in matters of religion, and concludes: "The defence only of the Church belongs to the magistrate. Had he once learnt not further to concern himself with Church affairs, half his labour might be spared and the commonwealth better tended." It is to be regretted that he had not entered upon this great subject at an earlier period. The little tract, addressed to the Republican members of Parliament, is designedly homely in style, and the magnificence of Milton's diction is still further tamed down by the necessity of resorting to dictation. It is nevertheless a powerful piece of argument, in its own sphere of abstract reason unanswerable, and only questionable in that lower sphere of expediency which Milton disdained. In the following August appeared a sequel with the sarcastic title, "Considerations on the likeliest means to remove Hirelings out of the Church." The recipe is simple and efficacious--cease to hire them, and they will cease to be hirelings. Suppress all ecclesiastical endowments, and let the clergyman be supported by free-will offerings. The fact that this would have consigned about half the established clergy to beggary does not trouble him; nor were they likely to be greatly troubled by a proposal so sublimely impracticable. Vested interests can only be over-ridden in times of revolution, and 1659, in outward appearance a year of anarchy, was in truth a year of reaction. For the rest, it is to be remarked that Milton scarcely allowed the ministry to be followed as a profession, and that his views on ecclesiastical organization had come to coincide very nearly with those now held by the Plymouth Brethren.

There is much plausibility in Pattison's comparison of the men of the Commonwealth disputing about matters of this sort on the eve of the Restoration, to the Greeks of Constantinople contending about the Azymite controversy while the Turks were breaching their walls. In fact, however, this blindness was not confined to one party. Anthony Wood, a Royalist, writing thirty years afterwards, speaks of the Restoration as an event which no man expected in September, 1659. The Commonwealth was no doubt dead as a Republic. "Pride's Purge," the execution of Charles, and Cromwell's expulsion of the remnant of the Commons, had long ago given it mortal wounds. It was not necessarily defunct as a Protectorate, or a renovated Monarchy: the history of England might have been very different if Oliver had bequeathed his power to Henry instead of to Richard. No such vigorous hand taking the helm, and the vessel of the State drifting more and more into anarchy, the great mass of Englishmen, to the frustration of many generous ideals, but to the credit of their practical good sense, pronounced for the restoration of Charles the Second. It is impossible to think without anger and grief of the declension which was to ensue, from Cromwell enforcing toleration for Protestants to Charles selling himself to France for a pension, from Blake at Tunis to the Dutch at Chatham. But the Restoration was no national apostasy. The people as a body did not decline from Milton's standard, for they had never attained to it; they did not accept the turpitudes of the new government, for they did not anticipate them. So far as sentiment inspired them, it was not love of license, but compassion for the misfortunes of an innocent prince. Common sense, however, had much more to do with prompting their action, and common sense plainly informed them that they had no choice between a restored king and a military despot. They would not have had even that if the leading military chief had not been a man of homely sense and vulgar aims; such an one as Milton afterwards drew in--

"Mammon, the least erected spirit that fell
From heaven, for even in heaven his looks and thoughts
Were always downward bent, admiring more
The riches of heaven's pavement, trodden gold."

In the field, or on the quarter-deck, George Monk was the stout soldier, acquitting himself of his military duty most punctually. In his political conduct he laid himself out for titles and money, as little of the ambitious usurper as of the self-denying patriot. Such are they for whom more generous spirits, imprudently forward in revolutions, usually find that they have laboured. "Great things," said Edward Gibbon Wakefield, "are begun by men with great souls and little breeches-pockets, and ended by men with great breeches-pockets and little souls."

Milton would not have been Milton if he could have acquiesced in an ever so needful Henry Cromwell or Charles Stuart. Never quick to detect the course of public opinion, he was now still further disabled by his blindness. There is great pathos in the thought of the sightless patriot hungering for tidings, "as the Red Sea for ghosts," and swayed hither and thither by the narratives and comments of passionate or interested reporters. At last something occurred which none could misunderstand or misrepresent. On February 11th, about ten at night, Mr. Samuel Pepys, being in Cheapside, heard "all the bells in all the churches a-ringing. But the common joy that was everywhere to be seen! The number of bonfires, there being fourteen between St. Dunstan's and Temple Bar, and at Strand Bridge I could at one view tell thirty-one fires. In King Street, seven or eight; and all around burning, roasting, and drinking for rumps. There being rumps tied upon sticks and carried up and down. The butchers at the May Pole in the Strand rang a merry peal with their knives when they were going to sacrifice their rump. On Ludgate Hill there was one turning of the spit that had a rump tied upon it, and another basting of it. Indeed, it was past imagination, both the greatness and the suddenness of it. At one end of the street you would think there was a whole lane of fire, and so hot that we were fain to keep on the further side." This burning of the Rump meant that the attempt of a miserable minority to pose as King, Lords, and Commons, had broken down, and that the restoration of Charles, for good or ill, was the decree of the people. A modern Republican might without disgrace have bowed to the gale, for such an one, unless hopelessly fanatical, denies the divine right of republics equally with that of kings, and allows no other title than that of the consent of the majority of citizens. But Milton had never admitted the rights of the majority: and in his supreme effort for the Republic, "The Ready and Easy Way to establish a free Commonwealth," he ignores the Royalist plurality, and assumes that the virtuous part of the nation, to whom alone he allows a voice, is as desirous as himself of the establishment of a Republic, and only needs to be shown the way. As this was by no means the case, the whole pamphlet rests upon sand: though in days when public opinion was guided not from the press but from the rostrum, many might have been won by the eloquence of Milton's invectives against the inhuman pride and hollow ceremonial of kingship, and his encomiums of the simple order when the ruler's main distinction from the ruled is the severity of his toil. "Whereas they who are the greatest are perpetual servants and drudges to the public at their own cost and charges, neglect their own affairs, yet are not elevated above their brethren; live soberly in their families, walk the street as other men, may be spoken to freely, familiarly, friendly without adoration." Whatever generous glow for equality such words might kindle, was only too likely to be quenched when the reader came to learn on what conditions Milton thought it attainable. His panacea was a permanent Parliament or Council of State, self-elected for life, or renewable at most only in definite proportions, at stated times. The whole history of England for the last twelve years was a commentary on the impotence of a Parliament that had outlived its mandate, and every line of the lesson had been lost upon Milton. He does indeed, near the end, betray a suspicion that the people may object to hand over the whole business of legislation to a self-elected and irresponsible body, and is led to make a remarkable suggestion, prefiguring the federal constitution of the United States, and in a measure the Home Rule and Communal agitations of our own day. He would make every county independent in so far as regards the execution of justice between man and man. The districts might make their own laws in this department, subject only to a moderate amount of control from the supreme council. This must have seemed to Milton's contemporaries the official enthronement of anarchy, and, in fact, his proposal, thrown off at a heat with the feverish impetuosity that characterizes the whole pamphlet, is only valuable as an aid to reflection. Yet, in proclaiming the superiority of healthy municipal life to a centralized administration, he has anticipated the judgment of the wisest publicists of our day, and shown a greater insight than was possessed by the more scientific statesmen of the eighteenth century.

One quality of Milton's pamphlet claims the highest admiration, its audacious courage. On the very eve of the Restoration, and with full though tardy recognition of its probable imminence, he protests as loudly as ever the righteousness of Charles's execution, and of the perpetual exclusion of his family from the throne. When all was lost, it was no disgrace to quit the field. His pamphlet appeared on March 3, 1660; a second edition, with considerable alterations, was for the time suppressed. On March 28th the publisher was imprisoned for vending treasonable books, among which the pamphlet was no doubt included. Every ensuing day added something to the discomfiture of the Republicans, until on May 1st, "the happiest May-day," says that ardent Royalist *du lendemain*, Pepys, "that hath been many a year to England," Charles II.'s letter was read to a Parliament that none could deny to have been freely chosen, and acclaimed, "without so much as one No." On May 7th, as is conjectured by the date of an assignment made to Cyriack Skinner as security for a loan, Milton quitted his house, and concealed himself in Bartholomew Close, Smithfield. Charles re-entered his kingdom on May 29th, and the hue and cry after regicides and their abettors began. The King had wisely left the business to Parliament, and, when the circumstances of the times, and the sincere horror in which good men held what they called regicide and sacrilege are duly considered, it must be owned that Parliament acted with humanity and moderation. Still, in the nature of things, proscription on a small scale was inevitable. Besides the regicides proper, twenty persons were to be named for imprisonment and permanent incapacitation for office then, and liable to prosecution and possibly capital punishment hereafter. It seemed almost inevitable that Milton should be included. On June 16th his writings against Charles I. were ordered to be burned by the hangman, which sentence was performed on August 27th. A Government proclamation enjoining their destruction had been issued on August 13th, and may now be read in the King's Library at the British Museum. He had not, then, escaped notice, and how he escaped proscription it is hard to say. Interest was certainly made for him. Andrew Marvell, Secretary Morrice, and Sir Thomas Clarges, Monk's brother-in-law, are named as active on his behalf; his brother and his nephew both belonged to the Royalist party, and there is a romantic story of Sir William Davenant having requited a like obligation under which he lay to Milton himself. More to his honour this than to have been the offspring of Shakespeare, but one tale is no better authenticated than the other. The simplest explanation is that twenty people were found more hated than Milton: it may also have seemed invidious to persecute a blind man. It is certainly remarkable that the authorities should have failed to find the hiding-place of so recognizable a person, if they really looked for it. Whether by his own adroitness or their connivance, he avoided arrest until the amnesty resolution of August 29th restored him to the world without even being incapacitated from office. He still had to run the gauntlet of the Serjeant-at-Arms, who at some period unknown arrested him as obnoxious to the resolution of June 16th, and detained him, charging exorbitant fees, until compelled to abate his demands by the Commons' resolution of December 15th. Milton relinquished his house in Westminster, and formed a temporary refuge on the north side of Holborn. His nerves were shaken; he started in his broken sleep with the apprehension and bewilderment natural to one for whom, physically and politically, all had become darkness.

His condition, in sooth, was one of well-nigh unmitigated misfortune, and his bearing up against it is not more of a proof of stoic fortitude than of innate cheerfulness. His cause lost, his ideals in the dust, his enemies triumphant, his friends dead on the scaffold, or exiled, or imprisoned, his name infamous, his principles execrated, his property seriously impaired by the vicissitudes of the times. He had been deprived of his appointment and salary as Latin Secretary, even before the Restoration: and he was now fleeced of two thousand pounds, invested in some kind of Government security, which was repudiated in spite of powerful intercession. Another "great sum" is said by Phillips to have been lost "by mismanagement and want of good advice," whether at this precise time is uncertain. The Dean and Chapter of Westminster reclaimed a considerable property which had passed out of their hands in the Civil War. The Serjeant-at-Arms had no doubt made all out of his captive that the Commons would let him. On the whole, Milton appears to have saved about L1500 from the wreck of his fortunes, and to have possessed about L200 income from the interest of this fund and other sources, destined to be yet further reduced within a few years. The value of money being then about three and a half times as great as now, this modest income was still a fair competence for one of his frugal habits, even when burdened with the care of three daughters. The history of his relations with these daughters is the saddest page of his life. "I looked that my vineyard should bring forth grapes, and it brought forth wild grapes." If any lot on earth could have seemed enviable to an imaginative mind and an affectionate heart, it would have been that of an Antigone or a Romola to a Milton. Milton's daughters chose to reject the fair repute that the simple fulfilment of evident duty would have brought them, and to be damned to everlasting fame, not merely as neglectful of their father, but as embittering his existence. The shocking speech attributed to one of them is, we may hope, not a fact; and it may not be true to the letter that they conspired to rob him, and sold his books to the ragpickers. The course of events down to his death, nevertheless, is sufficient evidence of the unhappiness of his household. Writing "Samson Agonistes" in calmer days, he lets us see how deep the iron had entered into his soul:

> "I dark in light exposed
> To daily fraud, contempt, abuse, and wrong,
> Within doors, or without, still as a fool
> In power of others, never in my own."

He probably never understood how greatly he was himself to blame. He had, in the first place, neglected to give his daughters the education which might have qualified them in some measure to appreciate him. The eldest, Anne, could not even write her name; and it is but a poor excuse to say that, though good-looking, she was deformed, and afflicted with an impediment in her speech. The second, Mary, who resembled her mother, and the third, Deborah, the most like her father, were better taught; but still not to the degree that could make them intelligent doers of the work they had to perform for him. They were so drilled in foreign languages, including Greek and Latin (Hebrew and Syriac are also mentioned, but this is difficult of belief), that they could read aloud to him without any comprehension of the meaning of the text. Sixty years afterwards, passages of Homer and Ovid were found lingering as melodious sounds in the memory of the youngest. Such a task, inexpressibly delightful to affection, must have been intolerably repulsive to dislike or indifference: we can scarcely wonder that two of these children (of the youngest we have a better report), abhorred the father who exacted so much and imparted so little. Yet, before visiting any of the parties with inexorable condemnation, we should consider the strong probability that much of the misery grew out of an antecedent state of things, for which none of them were responsible. The infant minds of two of the daughters, and the two chiefly named as undutiful, had been formed by their mother. Mistress Milton cannot have greatly cherished her husband, and what she wanted in love must have been made up in fear. She must have abhorred his principles and his writings, and probably gave free course to her feelings whenever she could have speech with a sympathizer, without caring whether the girls were within hearing. Milton himself, we know, was cheerful in congenial society, but he were no poet if he had not been reserved with the uncongenial. To them the silent, abstracted, often irritable, and finally sightless father would seem awful and forbidding. It is impossible to exaggerate the susceptibility of young minds to first impressions. The probability is that ere Mistress Milton departed this life, she had intentionally or unintentionally avenged all the injuries she could imagine herself to have received from her husband, and furnished him with a stronger argument than any that had found a place in the "Doctrine and Discipline of Divorce."

It is something in favour of the Milton girls that they were at least not calculating in their undutifulness. Had they reflected, they must have seen that their behaviour was little to their interest. If they brought a stepmother upon themselves, the blame was theirs. Something must certainly be done to keep Milton's library from the rag-women; and in February, 1663, by the advice of his excellent physician Dr. Paget, he married Elizabeth Minshull, daughter of a yeoman of Wistaston in Cheshire, a distant relation of Dr. Paget's own, and exactly thirty years younger than Milton. "A genteel person, a peaceful and agreeable woman," says Aubrey, who knew her, and refutes by anticipation Richardson's anonymous informant, perhaps Deborah Clarke, who libelled her as "a termagant." She was pretty, and had golden hair, which one connects pleasantly with the late sunshine she brought into Milton's life. She sang to his accompaniment on the organ and bass-viol, but is not recorded to have read or written for him; the only direct testimony we have of her care of him is his verbal acknowledgment of her attention to his creature comforts. Yet Aubrey's memoranda show that she could talk with her husband about Hobbes, and she treasured the letters he had received from distinguished foreigners. At the time of their marriage Milton was living in Jewin Street, Aldersgate, from which he soon afterwards removed to Artillery Walk, Bunhill Fields, his last residence. He lodged in the interim with Millington, the book auctioneer, a man of superior ability, whom an informant of Richardson's had often met in the streets leading his inmate by the hand.

It is at this era of Milton's history that we obtain the fullest details of his daily life, as being nearer to the recollection of those from whom information was sought after his death. His household was larger than might have been expected in his reduced circumstances; he had a man-servant, Greene, and a maid, named Fisher. That true hero-worshipper, Aubrey, tells us that he generally rose at four, and was even then attended by his "man" who read to him out of the Hebrew Bible. Such erudition in a serving-man almost surpasses credibility: the English Bible probably sufficed both. It is easier to believe that some one read to him or wrote for him from seven till dinner time: if, however, "the writing was nearly as much as the reading," much that Milton dictated must have been lost. His recreations were walking in his garden, never wanting to any of his residences, where he would continue for three or four hours at a time; swinging in a chair when weather prevented open-air exercise; and music, that blissful resource of blindness. His instrument was usually the organ, the counterpart of the stately harmony of his own verse. To these relaxations must be added the society of faithful friends, among whom Andrew Marvell, Dr. Paget, and Cyriack Skinner are particularly named. Nor did Edward Phillips neglect his uncle, finding him, as Aubrey implies, "most familiar and free in his conversation to those to whom most sour in his way of education." Milton had made him "a songster," and we can imagine the "sober, silent, and most harmless person" (Evelyn) opening his lips to accompany his uncle's music. Of Milton's manner Aubrey says, "Extreme pleasant in his conversation, and at dinner, supper, etc., but satirical." Visitors usually came from six till eight, if at all, and the day concluded with a light supper, sometimes of olives, which we may well imagine fraught for him with Tuscan memories, a pipe, and a glass of water. This picture of plain living and high thinking is confirmed by the testimony of the Quaker Thomas Ellwood, who for a short time read to him, and who describes the kindness of his demeanour, and the pains he took to teach the foreign method of pronouncing Latin. Even more; "having a curious ear, he understood by my tone when I understood what I read and when I did not, and accordingly would stop me, examine me, and open the most difficult passages to me." Milton must have felt a special tenderness for the Quakers, whose religious opinions, divested of the shell of eccentricity which the vulgar have always mistaken for the kernel, had become substantially his own. He had outgrown Independency as formerly Presbyterianism. His blindness served to excuse his absence from public worship; to which, so long at least as Clarendon's intolerance prevailed in the councils of Charles the Second, might be added the difficulty of finding edification in the pulpit, had he needed it. But these reasons, though not imaginary, were not those which really actuated him. He had ceased to value rites and forms of any kind, and, had his religious views been known, he would have been "equalled in fate" with his contemporary Spinoza. Yet he was writing a book which orthodox Protestantism has accepted as but a little lower than the Scriptures.

"The kingdom of heaven cometh not with observation." We know but little of the history of the greatest works of genius. That something more than usual should be known of "Paradise Lost" must be ascribed to the author's blindness, and consequent dependence upon amanuenses. When inspiration came upon him any one at hand would be called upon to preserve the precious verses, hence the progress of the poem was known to many, and Phillips can speak of "parcels of ten, twenty, or thirty verses at a time." We have already heard from him that Milton's season of inspiration lasted from the autumnal equinox to the vernal: the remainder of the year doubtless contributed much to the matter of his poem, if nothing to the form. His habits of composition appear to be shadowed forth by himself in the induction to the Third Book:--

"Thee, Sion, and the flowery brooks beneath
That wash thy hallowed feet, and warbling flow,
Nightly I visit--"

"Then feed on thoughts that voluntary move
Harmonious numbers; as the wakeful bird
Sings darkling, and in shadiest covert hid
Tunes her nocturnal note."

This is something more precise than a mere poetical allusion to his blindness, and the inference is strengthened by the anecdote that when "his celestial patroness" "Deigned nightly visitation unimplored," his daughters were frequently called at night to take down the verses, not one of which the whole world could have replaced. This was as it should be. Grand indeed is the thought of the unequalled strain poured forth when every other voice was hushed in the mighty city, to no meaner accompaniment than the music of the spheres. Respecting the date of composition, we may trust Aubrey's statement that the poem was commenced in 1658, and when the rapidity of Milton's composition is considered ("Easy my unpremeditated verse") it may, notwithstanding the terrible hindrances of the years 1659 and 1660, have been, as Aubrey thinks, completed by 1663. It would still require mature revision, which we know from Ellwood that it had received by the summer of 1665. Internal evidence of the chronology of the poem is very scanty. Professor Masson thinks that the first two books were probably written before the Restoration. In support of this view it may be urged that lines 500-505 of Book i. wear the appearance of an insertion after the Restoration, and that in the invocation to the Third Book Milton may be thought to allude to the dangers his life and liberty had afterwards encountered, figured by the regions of nether darkness which he had traversed as a poet.

> "Hail holy Light!...
> Thee I revisit now with bolder wing,
> Escaped the Stygian pool, though long detained
> In that obscure sojourn, while in my flight
> Through utter and through middle darkness borne."

The only other passage important in this respect is the famous one from the invocation to the Seventh Book, manifestly describing the poet's condition under the Restoration:--

> "Standing on earth, not rapt above the pole,
> More safe I sing with mortal voice, unchanged
> To hoarse or mute, though fallen on evil days,
> On evil days though fallen and evil tongues;
> In darkness, and with dangers compassed round,
> And solitude; yet not alone, while thou
> Visitest my slumbers nightly, or when morn
> Purples the east. Still govern thou my song,
> Urania, and fit audience find, though few.
> But drive far off the barbarous dissonance
> Of Bacchus and his revellers, the race
> Of that wild rout that tore the Thracian bard."

This allusion to the licentiousness of the Restoration literature could hardly have been made until its tendencies had been plainly developed. At this time "Paradise Lost" was half finished. ("Half yet remains unsung.") The remark permits us to conclude that Milton conceived and executed his poem as a whole, going steadily through it, and not leaving gaps to be supplied at higher or lower levels of inspiration. There is no evidence of any resort to older material, except in the case of Satan's address to the Sun.

The publication of "Paradise Lost" was impeded like the birth of Hercules. In

1665 London was a city of the dying and the dead; in 1666 the better part of it was laid in ashes. One remarkable incident of the calamity was the destruction of the stocks of the booksellers, which had been brought into the vaults of St. Paul's for safety, and perished with the cathedral. "Paradise Lost" might have easily, like its hero--

> "In the singing smoke
> Uplifted spurned the ground."

but the negotiations for its publication were not complete until April 27, 1667, on which day John Milton, "in consideration of five pounds to him now paid by Samuel Symmons, and other the considerations herein mentioned," assigned to the said Symmons, "all that book, copy, or manuscript of a poem intituled 'Paradise Lost,' or by whatsoever ether title or name the same is or shall be called or distinguished, now lately licensed to be printed." The other considerations were the payment of the like sum of five pounds upon the entire sale of each of the first three impressions, each impression to consist of thirteen hundred copies. "According to the present value of money," says Professor Masson, "it was as if Milton had received L17 10s. down, and was to expect L70 in all. That was on the supposition of a sale of 3,900 copies." He lived to receive ten pounds altogether; and his widow in 1680 parted with all her interest in the copyright for eight pounds, Symmons shortly afterwards reselling it for twenty-five. He is not, therefore, to be enumerated among those publishers who have fattened upon their authors, and when the size of the book and the unfashionableness of the writer are considered, his enterprise may perhaps appear the most remarkable feature of the transaction. As for Milton, we may almost rejoice that he should have reaped no meaner reward than immortality.

It will have been observed that in the contract with Symmons "Paradise Lost" is said to have been "lately licensed to be printed." The censorship named in "Areopagitica" still prevailed, with the difference that prelates now sat in judgment upon Puritans. The Archbishop gave or refused license through his chaplains, and could not be ignored as Milton had ignored the little Presbyterian Popes; Geneva in his person must repair to Lambeth. Chaplain Tomkyns, who took cognisance of

"Paradise Lost," was fortunately a broad-minded man, disposed to live and let live, though scrupling somewhat when he found "perplexity" and "fear of change" imputed to "monarchs." His objections were overcome, and on August 20, 1667--three weeks after the death of Cowley, and eight days after Pepys had heard the deceased extolled as the greatest of English poets--John Milton came forth clad as with adamantine mail in the approbation of Thomas Tomkyns. The moment beseemed the event, it was a crisis in English history, when heaven's "golden scales" for weighing evil against good were hung--

"Betwixt Astrea and the Scorpion sign,"

one weighted with a consuming fleet, the other with a falling minister. The Dutch had just burned the English navy at Chatham; on the other hand, the reign of respectable bigotry was about to pass away with Clarendon. Far less reputable men were to succeed, but men whose laxity of principle at least excluded intolerance. The people were on the move, if not, as Milton would have wished, "a noble and puissant nation rousing herself like a strong man after sleep," at least a faint and weary nation creeping slowly--Tomkyns and all--towards an era of liberty and reason when Tomkyns's imprimatur would be accounted Tomkyns's impertinence.

CHAPTER VII.

The world's great epics group themselves in two divisions, which may be roughly defined as the natural and the artificial. The spontaneous or self-created epic is a confluence of traditions, reduced to symmetry by the hand of a master. Such are the Iliad, the Odyssey, the great Indian and Persian epics, the Nibelungen Lied. In such instances it may be fairly said that the theme has chosen the poet, rather than the poet the theme. When the epic is a work of reflection, the poet has deliberately selected his subject, and has not, in general, relied so much upon the wealth of pre-existing materials as upon the capabilities of a single circumstance. Such are the epics of Virgil, Camoens, Tasso, Milton; Dante, perhaps, standing alone as the one epic poet (for we cannot rank Ariosto and Spenser in this class) who owes everything but his creed to his own invention. The traditional epic, created by the people and only moulded by the minstrel, is so infinitely the more important for the history of culture, that, since this new field of investigation has become one of paramount interest, the literary epic has been in danger of neglect. Yet it must be allowed that to evolve an epic out of a single incident is a greater intellectual achievement than to weave one out of a host of ballads. We must also admit that, leaving the unique Dante out of account, Milton essayed a more arduous enterprise than any of his predecessors, and in this point of view may claim to stand above them all. We are so accustomed to regard the existence of "Paradise Lost" as an ultimate fact, that we but imperfectly realize the gigantic difficulty and audacity of the undertaking. To paint the bloom of Paradise with the same brush that has depicted the flames and blackness of the nether world; to make the Enemy of Mankind, while preserving this character, an heroic figure, not without claims on sympathy and admiration; to lend fit speech to the father and mother of humanity, to angels and archangels, and even Deity itself;--these achievements required a Michael Angelo shorn of his strength in every other province of art, that all might be concentrated in song.

It is easy to represent "Paradise Lost" as obsolete by pointing out that its demonology and angelology have for us become mere mythology. This criticism is more formidable in appearance than in reality. The vital question for the poet is his own belief, not the belief of his readers. If the Iliad has survived not merely the decay of faith in the Olympian divinities, but the criticism which has pulverized Achilles as a historical personage, "Paradise Lost" need not be much affected by general disbelief in the personality of Satan, and universal disbelief in that of Gabriel, Raphael, and Uriel. A far more vulnerable point is the failure of the purpose so ostentatiously proclaimed, "To justify the ways of God to men." This problem was absolutely insoluble on Milton's data, except by denying the divine foreknowledge, a course not open to him. The conduct of the Deity who allows his adversary to ruin his innocent creature from the purely malignant motive

"That with reiterated crimes he might
Heap on himself damnation,"

without further interposition than a warning which he foresees will be fruitless, implies a grievous deficiency either in wisdom or in goodness, or at best falsifies the declaration:

"Necessity and chance
Approach me not, and what I will is fate."

The like flaw runs through the entire poem, where Satan alone is resolute and rational. Nothing can exceed the imbecility of the angelic guard to which Man's defence is entrusted. Uriel, after threatening to drag Satan in chains back to Tartarus, and learning by a celestial portent that he actually has the power to fulfil his threat, considerately draws the fiend's attention to the circumstance, and advises him to take himself off, which Satan judiciously does, with the intention of returning as soon as convenient. The angels take all possible pains to prevent his gaining an entrance into Paradise, but omit to keep Adam and Eve themselves in sight, notwithstanding the strong hint they have received by finding the intruder

> "Squat like a toad, close at the ear of Eve,
> Assaying by his devilish art to reach
> The organs of her fancy, and with them forge
> Illusions as he list, phantasms and dreams."

If anything more infatuated can be imagined, it is the simplicity of the All-Wise Himself in entrusting the wardership of the gate of Hell, and consequently the charge of keeping Satan *in*, to the beings in the universe most interested in letting him *out*. The sole but sufficient excuse is that these faults are inherent in the subject. If Milton had not thought that he could justify the ways of Jehovah to man he would not have written at all; common sense on the part of the angels would have paralysed the action of the poem; we should, if conscious of our loss, have lamented the irrefragable criticism that should have stifled the magnificent allegory of Sin and Death. Another critical thrust is equally impossible to parry. It is true that the Evil One is the hero of the epic. Attempts have been made to invest Adam with this character. He is, indeed, a great figure to contemplate, and such as might represent the ideal of humanity till summoned to act and suffer. When, indeed, he partakes of the forbidden fruit in disobedience to his Maker, but in compassion to his mate, he does seem for a moment to fulfil the canon which decrees that the hero shall not always be faultless, but always shall be noble. The moment, however, that he begins to wrangle with Eve about their respective shares of blame, he forfeits his estate of heroism more irretrievably than his estate of holiness--a fact of which Milton cannot have been unaware, but he had no liberty to forsake the Scripture narrative. Satan remains, therefore, the only possible hero, and it is one of the inevitable blemishes of the poem that he should disappear almost entirely from the latter books.

These defects, and many more which might be adduced, are abundantly compensated by the poet's vital relation to the religion of his age. No poet whose fame is co-extensive with the civilised world, except Shakespeare and Goethe, has ever been greatly in advance of his times. Had Milton been so, he might have avoided many faults, but he would not have been a representative poet; nor could Shelley have classed him with Homer and Dante, and above Virgil, as "the third epic poet; that is, the third poet the series of whose creations bore a defined and intelligible relation to the knowledge and sentiment and religion of the age in which he lived, and of the ages which followed it, developing itself in correspondence with their development." Hence it is that in the "Adonais," Shelley calls Milton "the third among the sons of light."

A clear conception of the universe as Milton's inner eye beheld it, and of his religious and philosophical opinions in so far as they appear in the poem, is indispensable for a correct understanding of "Paradise Lost." The best service to be rendered to the reader within such limits as ours is to direct him to Professor Masson's discussion of Milton's cosmology in his "Life of Milton," and also in his edition of the Poetical Works. Generally speaking, it may be said that Milton's conception of the universe is Ptolemaic, that for him sun and moon and planets revolve around the central earth, rapt by the revolution of the crystal spheres in which, sphere enveloping sphere, they are successively located. But the light which had broken in upon him from the discoveries of Galileo has led him to introduce features not irreconcilable with the solar centre and ethereal infinity of Copernicus; so that "the poet would expect the effective permanence of his work in the imagination of the world, whether Ptolemy or Copernicus should prevail." So Professor Masson, who finely and justly adds that Milton's blindness helped him "by having already converted all external space in his own sensations into an infinite of circumambient blackness through which he could flash brilliance at his pleasure." His inclination as a thinker is evidently towards the Copernican theory, but he saw that the Ptolemaic, however inferior in sublimity, was better adapted to the purpose of a poem requiring a definite theatre of action. For rapturous contemplation of the glory of God in nature, the Copernican system is immeasurably the more stimulating to the spirit, but when made the theatre of an action the universe fatigues with its infinitude--

"Millions have meaning; after this
Cyphers forget the integer."

An infinite sidereal universe would have stultified the noble description how Satan--

"In the emptier waste, resembling air,
Weighs his spread wings, at leisure to behold
Far off the empyreal heaven, extended wide
In circuit, undetermined square or round,
With opal towers and battlements adorned
Of living sapphire, once his native seat;
And fast by, hanging in a golden chain,
This pendant world, in bigness as a star
Of smallest magnitude close by the moon."

This pendant world, observe, is not the earth, as Addison understood it, but the entire sidereal universe, depicted not as the infinity we now know it to be, but as a definite object, so insulated in the vastness of space as to be perceptible to the distant Fiend as a minute star, and no larger in comparison with the courts of Heaven--themselves not wholly seen--than such a twinkler matched with the full-orbed moon. Such a representation, if it diminishes the grandeur of the universe accessible to sense, exalts that of the supersensual and extramundane regions where the action takes its birth, and where Milton's gigantic imagination is most perfectly at home.

There is no such compromise between religious creeds in Milton's mind as he saw good to make between Ptolemy and Copernicus. The matter was, in his estimation, far too serious. Never was there a more unaccountable misstatement than Ruskin's, that "Paradise Lost" is a poem in which every artifice of invention is consciously employed--not a single fact being conceived as tenable by any living faith. Milton undoubtedly believed most fully in the actual existence of all his chief personages, natural and supernatural, and was sure that, however he might have indulged his imagination in the invention of incidents, he had represented character with the fidelity of a conscientious historian. His religious views, moreover, are such as he could never have thought it right to publish if he had not been intimately convinced of their truth. He has strayed far from the creed of Puritanism. He is an Arian; his Son of God, though an unspeakably exalted being, is dependent, inferior, not self-existent, and could be merged in the Father's person or obliterated entirely without the least diminution of Almighty perfection. He is, moreover, no longer a Calvinist: Satan and Adam both possess free will, and neither need have fallen. The reader must accept these views, as well as Milton's conception of the materiality of the spiritual world, if he is to read to good purpose. "If his imagination," says Pattison, pithily, "is not active enough to assist the poet, he must at least not resist him."

This is excellent advice as respects the general plan of "Paradise Lost," the materiality of its spiritual personages, and its system of philosophy and theology. Its poetical beauties can only be resisted where they are not perceived. They have repeated the miracles of Orpheus and Amphion, metamorphosing one most bitterly obnoxious, of whom so late as 1687 a royalist wrote that "his fame is gone out like a candle in a snuff, and his memory will always stink," into an object of universal veneration. From the first instant of perusal the imagination is led in captivity, and for the first four books at least stroke upon stroke of sublimity follows with such continuous and undeviating regularity that sublimity seems this Creation's first law, and we feel like pigmies transported to a world of giants. There is nothing forced or affected in this grandeur, no visible effort, no barbaric profusion, everything proceeds with a severe and majestic order, controlled by the strength that called it into being. The similes and other poetical ornaments, though inexpressibly magnificent, seem no more so than the greatness of the general conception demands. Grant that Satan in his fall is not "less than archangel ruined," and it is no exaggeration but the simplest truth to depict his mien--

"As when the sun, new risen,
Looks through the horizontal misty air,
Shorn of his beams; or from behind the moon,
In dim eclipse, disastrous twilight sheds
On half the nations."

When such a being voyages through space it is no hyperbole to compare him to a whole fleet, judiciously shown at such distance as to suppress every minute detail that could diminish the grandeur of the image--

"As when far off at sea a fleet descried
Hangs in the clouds, by equinoctial winds
Close sailing from Bengala, or the isles
Of Ternate and Tidore, whence merchants bring
Their spicy drugs: they on the trading flood,
Through the wide Ethiopian to the Cape,
Ply stemming nightly towards the pole: so seemed
Far off the flying Fiend."

These similes, and an infinity of others, are grander than anything in Homer, who would, however, have equalled them with an equal subject. Dante's treatment is altogether different; the microscopic intensity of perception in which he so far surpasses Homer and Milton affords, in our opinion, no adequate compensation for his inferiority in magnificence. That the theme of "Paradise Lost" should have evoked such grandeur is a sufficient compensation for its incurable flaws and the utter breakdown of its ostensible moral purpose. There is yet another department of the poem where Milton writes as he could have written on nothing else. The elements of his under-world are comparatively simple, fire and darkness, fallen angels now huddled thick as leaves in Vallombrosa; anon,

"A forest huge of spears and thronging helms,"
charming their painful steps over the burning marl by

"The Dorian mood
Of flutes and soft recorders;"

the dazzling magnificence of Pandemonium; the ineffable welter of Chaos; proudly eminent over all like a tower, the colossal personality of Satan. The description of Paradise and the story of Creation, if making less demand on the poet's creative power, required greater resources of knowledge, and more consummate skill in combination. Nature must yield up her treasures, whatever of fair and stately the animal and vegetable kingdoms can afford must be brought together, blended in gorgeous masses or marshalled in infinite procession. Here Milton is as profuse as he has hitherto been severe, and with good cause; it is possible to make Hell too repulsive for art, it is not possible to make Eden too enchanting. In his descriptions of the former the effect is produced by a perpetual succession of isolated images of awful majesty; in his Paradise and Creation the universal landscape is bathed in a general atmosphere of lustrous splendour. This portion of his work is accordingly less great in detached passages, but is little inferior in general greatness. No less an authority than Tennyson, indeed, expresses a preference for the "bowery loneli-ness" of Eden over the "Titan angels" of the "deep-domed Empyrean." If this only means that Milton's Eden is finer than his war in heaven, we must concur; but if a wider application be intended, it does seem to us that his Pandemonium exalts him to a greater height above every other poet than his Paradise exalts him above his predecessor, and in some measure, his exemplar, Spenser.

To remain at such an elevation was impossible. Milton compares unfavour-ably with Homer in this; his epic begins at its zenith, and after a while visibly and continually declines. His genius is unimpaired, but his skill transcends his stuff. The fall of man and its consequences could not by any device be made as interest-ing as the fall of Satan, of which it is itself but a consequence. It was, moreover, absolutely inevitable that Adam's fall, the proper catastrophe of the poem, should occur some time before the conclusion, otherwise there would have been no space for the unfolding of the scheme of Redemption, equally essential from the point of view of orthodoxy and of art. The effect is the same as in the case of Shakespeare's "Julius Caesar," which, having proceeded with matchless vigour up to the flight of the conspirators after Antony's speech, becomes comparatively tame and languid, and cannot be revived even by such a masterpiece as the contention between Bru-tus and Cassius. It is to be regretted that Milton's extreme devotion to the letter of Scripture has not permitted him to enrich his latter books with any corresponding episode. It is not until the very end that he is again truly himself--

"They, looking back, all the eastern side beheld
Of Paradise, so late their happy seat,
Waved over by that flaming brand; the gate
With dreadful faces thronged and fiery arms.
Some natural tears they dropped, but wiped them soon.

> The world was all before them, where to choose
> Their place of rest, and Providence their guide.
> They, hand in hand, with wandering steps and slow,
> Through Eden took their solitary way."

Some minor objections may be briefly noticed. The materiality of Milton's celestial warfare has been censured by every one from the days of Sir Samuel Morland,[6] a splenetic critic, who had incurred Milton's contempt by his treachery to Cromwell and Thurloe. Warfare, however, there must be: war cannot be made without weapons; and Milton's only fault is that he has rather exaggerated than minimized the difficulties of his subject. A sense of humour would have spiked his celestial artillery, but a lively perception of the ridiculous is scarcely to be demanded from a Milton. After all, he was borrowing from good poets,[7] whose thought in itself is correct, and even profound; it is only when artillery antedates humanity that the ascription of its invention to the Tempter seems out of place. The metamorphosis of the demons into serpents has been censured as grotesque; but it was imperatively necessary to manifest by some unmistakable outward sign that victory did not after all remain with Satan, and the critics may be challenged to find one more appropriate. The bridge built by Sin and Death is equally essential. Satan's progeny must not be dismissed without some exploit worthy of their parentage. The one passage where Milton's taste seems to us entirely at fault is the description of the Paradise of Fools (iii., 481-497), where his scorn of--

> "Reliques, beads,
> Indulgences, dispenses, pardons, bulls,"

has tempted him to chequer the sublime with the ludicrous.

No subject but a Biblical one would have insured Milton universal popularity among his countrymen, for his style is that of an ancient classic transplanted, like Aladdin's palace set down with all its magnificence in the heart of Africa; and his diction, the delight of the educated, is the despair of the ignorant man. Not that this diction is in any respect affected or pedantic. Milton was the darling poet of our greatest modern master of unadorned Saxon speech, John Bright. But it is freighted with classic allusion--not alone from the ancient classics--and comes to us rich with gathered sweets, like a wind laden with the scent of many flowers. "It is," says Pattison, "the elaborated outcome of all the best words of all antecedent poetry-- the language of one who lives in the companionship of the great and the wise of past time." "Words," the same writer reminds us, "over and above their dictionary signification, connote all the feeling which has gathered round them by reason of their employment through a hundred generations of song." So it is, every word seems instinct with its own peculiar beauty, and fraught with its own peculiar association, and yet each detail is strictly subordinate to the general effect. No poet of Milton's rank, probably, has been equally indebted to his predecessors, not only for his vocabulary, but for his thoughts. Reminiscences throng upon him, and he takes all that comes, knowing that he can make it lawfully his own. The comparison of Satan's shield to the moon, for instance, is borrowed from the similar comparison of the shield of Achilles in the Iliad, but what goes in Homer comes out Milton. Homer merely says that the huge and massy shield emitted a lustre like that of the moon in heaven. Milton heightens the resemblance by giving the shield shape, calls in the telescope to endow it with what would seem preternatural dimensions to the naked eye, and enlarges even these by the suggestion of more than the telescope can disclose--

"His ponderous shield,
Ethereal temper, massy, large, and round
Behind him cast; the broad circumference
Hung on his shoulders like the moon, whose orb
Through optic glass the Tuscan artist views
At evening, from the top of Fesole,
Or in Valdarno, to descry new lands,
Rivers or mountains in her spotty globe."

Thus does Milton appropriate the wealth of past literature, secure of being able to recoin it with his own image and superscription. The accumulated learning which might have choked the native fire of a feebler spirit was but nourishment to his. The polished stones and shining jewels of his superb mosaic are often borrowed, but its plan and pattern are his own.

One of the greatest charms of "Paradise Lost" is the incomparable metre, which, after Coleridge and Tennyson have done their utmost, remains without equal in our language for the combination of majesty and music. It is true that this majesty is to a certain extent inherent in the subject, and that the poet who could rival it would scarcely be well advised to exert his power to the full unless his theme also rivalled the magnificence of Milton's. Milton, on his part, would have been quite content to have written such blank verse as Wordsworth's "Yew Trees," or as the exordium of "Alastor," or as most of Coleridge's idylls, had his subject been less than epical. The organ-like solemnity of his verbal music is obtained partly by extreme attention to variety of pause, but chiefly, as Wordsworth told Klopstock, and as Mr. Addington Symonds points out more at length, by the period, not the individual line, being made the metrical unit, "so that each line in a period shall carry its proper burden of sound, but the burden shall be differently distributed in the successive verses." Hence lines which taken singly seem almost unmetrical, in combination with their associates appear indispensable parts of the general harmony. Mr. Symonds gives some striking instances. Milton's versification is that of a learned poet, profound in thought and burdened with the further care of ordering his thoughts: it is therefore only suited to sublimity of a solemn or meditative cast, and most unsuitable to render the unstudied sublimity of Homer. Perhaps no passage is better adapted to display its dignity, complicated artifice, perpetual retarding movement, concerted harmony, and grave but ravishing sweetness than the description of the coming on of Night in the Fourth Book:--

> "Now came still evening on, and twilight grey
> Had in her sober livery all things clad;
> Silence accompanied; for beast and bird,
> They to their grassy couch, these to their nests,
> Were slunk, all but the wakeful nightingale;
> She all night long her amorous descant sung;
> Silence was pleased: now glowed the firmament
> With living sapphires; Hesperus that led
> The stary host rose brightest, till the moon,

Rising in clouded majesty, at length
Apparent queen unveiled her peerless light,
And o'er the dark her silver mantle threw."

How exquisite the indication of the pauseless continuity of the nightingale's song by the transition from short sentences, cut up by commas and semicolons, to the "linked sweetness long drawn out" of "She all night long her amorous descant sung"! The poem is full of similar felicities, none perhaps more noteworthy than the sequence of monosyllables that paints the enormous bulk of the prostrate Satan:--

"So stretched out huge in length the Arch-fiend lay."

It is a most interesting subject for inquiry from what sources, other than the Scriptures, Milton drew aid in the composition of "Paradise Lost." The most striking counterpart is Calderon, to whom he owed as little as Calderon can have owed to him. "El Magico Prodigioso," already cited as affording a remarkable parallel to "Comus," though performed in 1637, was not printed until 1663, when "Paradise Lost" was already completed.[8] The two great religious poets have naturally conceived the Evil One much in the same manner, and Calderon's Lucifer,

"Like the red outline of beginning Adam,"
might well have passed as the original draft of Milton's Satan:--

"In myself I am
A world of happiness and misery;
This I have lost, and that I must lament
For ever. In my attributes I stood
So high and so heroically great,
In lineage so supreme, and with a genius
Which penetrated with a glance the world
Beneath my feet, that, won by my high merit,
A King--whom I may call the King of Kings,
Because all others tremble in their pride

Before the terrors of his countenance--
In his high palace, roofed with brightest gems
Of living light--call them the stars of heaven--
Named me his counsellor. But the high praise
Stung me with pride and envy, and I rose
In mighty competition, to ascend
His seat, and place my foot triumphantly
Upon his subject thrones. Chastised, I know
The depth to which ambition falls. For mad
Was the attempt; and yet more mad were now
Repentance of the irrevocable deed.
Therefore I chose this ruin with the glory
Of not to be subdued, before the shame
Of reconciling me with him who reigns
By coward cession. Nor was I alone,
Nor am I now, nor shall I be, alone.
And there was hope, and there may still be hope;
For many suffrages among his vassals
Hailed me their lord and king, and many still
Are mine, and many more perchance shall be."

A striking proof that resemblance does not necessarily imply plagiarism. Milton's affinity to Calderon has been overlooked by his commentators; but four luminaries have been named from which he is alleged to have drawn, however sparingly, in his golden urn--Caedmon, the Adamus Exul of Grotius, the Adamo of the Italian dramatist Andreini, and the Lucifer of the Dutch poet Vondel. Caedmon, first printed in 1655, it is but barely possible that he should have known, and ere he could have known him the conception of "Paradise Lost" was firmly implanted in his mind. External evidence proves his acquaintance with Grotius, internal evidence his knowledge of Andreini: and small as are his direct obligations to the Italian drama, we can easily believe with Hayley that "his fancy caught fire from that spirited, though irregular and fantastic composition." Vondel's Lucifer--whose subject is not the fall of Adam, but the fall of Satan--was acted and published in

1654, when Milton is known to have been studying Dutch, but when the plan of "Paradise Lost" must have been substantially formed. There can, nevertheless, be no question of the frequent verbal correspondences, not merely between Vondel's Lucifer and "Paradise Lost," but between his Samson and "Samson Agonistes." Milton's indebtedness, so long ago as 1829, attracted the attention of an English poet of genius, Thomas Lovell Beddoes, who pointed out that his lightning-speech, "Better to reign in hell than serve in heaven," was a thunderbolt condensed from a brace of Vondel's clumsy Alexandrines, which Beddoes renders thus:--

"And rather the first prince at an inferior court
Than in the blessed light the second or still less."

Mr. Gosse followed up the inquiry, which eventually became the subject of a monograph by Mr. George Edmundson ("Milton and Vondel," 1885). That Milton should have had, as he must have had, Vondel's works translated aloud to him, is a most interesting proof, alike of his ardour in the enrichment of his own mind, and of his esteem for the Dutch poet. Although, however, his obligations to predecessors are not to be overlooked, they are in general only for the most obvious ideas and expressions, lying right in the path of any poet treating the subject. *Je l'aurais bien pris sans toi.* When, as in the instance above quoted, he borrows anything more recondite, he so exalts and transforms it that it passes from the original author to him like an angel the former has entertained unawares. This may not entirely apply to the Italian reformer, Bernardino Ochino, to whom, rather than to Tasso, Milton seems indebted for the conception of his diabolical council. Ochino, in many respects a kindred spirit to Milton, must have been well known to him as the first who had dared to ventilate the perilous question of the lawfulness of polygamy. In Ochino's "Divine Tragedy," which he may have read either in the Latin original or in the nervous translation of Bishop Poynet, Milton would find a hint for his infernal senate. "The introduction to the first dialogue," says Ochino's biographer Benrath, "is highly dramatic, and reminds us of Job and Faust." Ochino's arch-fiend, like Milton's, announces a masterstroke of genius. "God sent His Son into the world, and I will send my son." Antichrist accordingly comes to light in the shape of the Pope, and works infinite havoc until Henry VIII. is divinely commissioned for his discomfiture. It is a token, not only of Milton's, but of Vondel's, indebtedness, that, with Ochino as with them, Beelzebub holds the second place in the council, and even admonishes his leader. "I fear me," he remarks, "lest when Antichrist shall die, and come down hither to hell, that as he passeth us in wickedness, so he will be above us in dignity." Prescience worthy of him who

> "In his rising seemed
> A pillar of state; deep on his front engraven
> Deliberation sat, and public care;
> And princely counsel in his face yet shone."

Milton's borrowings, nevertheless, nowise impair his greatness. The obligation is rather theirs, of whose stores he has condescended to avail himself. He may be compared to his native country, which, fertile originally in little but enterprise, has made the riches of the earth her own. He has given her a national epic, inferior to no other, and unlike most others, founded on no merely local circumstance, but such as must find access to every nation acquainted with the most widely-circulated Book in the world. He has further enriched his native literature with an imperishable monument of majestic diction, an example potent to counteract that wasting agency of familiar usage by which language is reduced to vulgarity, as sea-water wears cliffs to shingle. He has reconciled, as no other poet has ever done, the Hellenic spirit with the Hebraic, the Bible with the Renaissance. And, finally, as we began by saying, his poem is the mighty bridge--

> "Bound with Gorgonian rigour not to move,"

across which the spirit of ancient poetry has travelled to modern times, and by which the continuity of great English literature has remained unbroken.

CHAPTER VIII.

In recording the publication of "Paradise Lost" in 1667, we have passed over
the interval of Milton's life immediately subsequent to the completion of the
poem in 1663. The first incident of any importance is his migration to Chalfont St. Giles, near Beaconsfield, in Buckinghamshire, about July, 1665, to
escape the plague then devastating London. Ell wood, whose family lived in the
neighbourhood of Chalfont, had at his request taken for him "a pretty box" in that
village; and we are, says Professor Masson, "to imagine Milton's house in Artillery
Walk shuttered up, and a coach and a large waggon brought to the door, and the
blind man helped in, and the wife and the three daughters following, with a servant
to look after the books and other things they have taken with them, and the whole
party driven away towards Giles-Chalfont." According to the same authority, Chalfont well deserves the name of Sleepy Hollow, lying at the bottom of a leafy dell.
Milton's cottage, alone of his residences, still exists, though divided into two tene-
ments. It is a two-storey dwelling, with a garden, is built of brick, with wooden
beams, musters nine rooms--though a question arises whether some of them ought
not rather to be described as closets; the porch in which Milton may have breathed
the summer air is gone, but the parlour retains the latticed casement at which he
sat, though through it he could not see. His infirmity rendered the confined situation less of a drawback, and there are abundance of pleasant lanes, along which he
could be conducted in his sightless strolls:--

"As one who long in populous city pent,
Where houses thick and sewers annoy the air,
Forth issuing on a summer's morn to breathe
Among the pleasant villages and farms

Adjoined, from each new thing conceives delight,
The smell of grain, or tedded grass, or kine,
Or dairy, each rural sight, each rural sound."

Milton was probably no stranger to the neighbourhood, having lived within thirteen miles of it when he dwelt at Horton. Ellwood could not welcome him on his arrival, being in prison on account of an affray at what should have been the paragon of decorous solemnities--a Quaker funeral. When released, about the end of August or the beginning of September, he waited upon Milton, who, "after some discourses, called for a manuscript of his; which he delivered to me, bidding me take it home with me and read it at my leisure. When I set myself to read it, I found it was that excellent poem which he entitled 'Paradise Lost.'" Professor Masson justly remarks that Milton would not have trusted the worthy Quaker adolescent with the only copy of his epic; we may be sure, therefore, that other copies existed, and that the poem was at this date virtually completed and ready for press. When the manuscript was returned, Ellwood, after "modestly, but freely, imparting his judgment," observed, "Thou hast said much here of Paradise Lost, but what hast thou to say of Paradise Found? He made no answer, but sat some time in a muse; then brake off that discourse, and fell on another subject." The plague was then at its height, and did not abate sufficiently for Milton to return to town with safety until about February in the following year, leaving, it has been asserted, a record of himself at Chalfont in the shape of a sonnet on the pestilence regarded as a judgment for the sins of the King, written with a diamond on a window-pane--as if the blind poet could write even with a pen! The verses, nevertheless, may not impossibly be genuine: they are almost too Miltonic for an imitator between 1665 and 1738, when they were first published.

The public calamity of 1666 affected Milton more nearly than that of 1665. The Great Fire came within a quarter of a mile of his house, and though he happily escaped the fate of Shirley, and did not make one of the helpless crowd of the homeless and destitute, his means were seriously abridged by the destruction of the house in Bread Street where he had first seen the light, and which he had retained through all the vicissitudes of his fortunes. He could not, probably, have published "Paradise Lost" without the co-operation of Samuel Symmons. Symmons's endeavours to push the sale of the book make the bibliographical history of the first edition unusually interesting. There were at least nine different issues, as fresh batches were successively bound up, with frequent alterations of title-page as reasonable cause became apparent to the strategic Symmons. First Milton's name is given in full, then he is reduced to initials, then restored; Symmons's own name, at first suppressed, by and by appears; his agents are frequently changed; and the title is altered to suit the year of issue, that the book may seem a novelty. The most important of all these alterations is one in which the author must have actively participated--the introduction of the Argument which, a hundred and forty years afterwards, was to cause Harriet Martineau to take up "Paradise Lost" at the age of seven, and of the Note on the metre conveying "a reason of that which stumbled many, why this poem rimes not." Partly, perhaps, by help of these devices, certainly without any aid from advertising or reviewing, the impression of thirteen hundred copies was disposed of within twenty months, as attested by Milton's receipt for his second five pounds, April 26, 1669--two years, less one day, since the signature of the original contract. The first printed notice appeared after the edition had been entirely sold. It was by Milton's nephew, Edward Phillips, and was contained in a little Latin essay appended to Buchlerus's "Treasury of Poetical Phrases."

"John Milton, in addition to other most elegant writings of his,
both in English and Latin, has recently published 'Paradise Lost,'
a poem which, whether we regard the sublimity of the subject, or
the combined pleasantness and majesty of the style, or the
sublimity of the invention, or the beauty of its images and
descriptions of nature, will, if I mistake not, receive the name
of truly heroic, inasmuch as by the suffrages of many not
unqualified to judge, it is reputed to have reached the perfection
of this kind of poetry."

The "many not unqualified" undoubtedly included the first critic of the age, Dryden. Lord Buckhurst is also named as an admirer--pleasing anecdotes respecting the practical expression of his admiration, and of Sir John Denham's, seem apocryphal.

While "Paradise Lost" was thus slowly upbearing its author to the highest heaven of fame, Milton was achieving other titles to renown, one of which he deemed nothing inferior. We shall remember Ellwood's hint that he might find something to say about Paradise Found, and the "muse" into which it cast him. When, says the Quaker, he waited upon Milton after the latter's return to London, Milton "showed me his second poem, called 'Paradise Regained,' and in a pleasant tone said to me, 'This is owing to you; for you put it into my head by the question you put to me at Chalfont; which before I had not thought of.'" Ellwood does not tell us the date of this visit, and Phillips may be right in believing that "Paradise Regained" was entirely composed after the publication of "Paradise Lost"; but it seems unlikely that the conception should have slumbered so long in Milton's mind, and the most probable date is between Michaelmas, 1665, and Lady-day, 1666. Phillips records that Milton could never hear with patience "Paradise Regained" "censured to be much inferior" to "Paradise Lost." "The most judicious," he adds, agreed with him, while allowing that "the subject might not afford such variety of invention," which was probably all that the injudicious meant. There is no external evidence of the date of his next and last poem, "Samson Agonistes," but its development of Miltonic mannerisms would incline us to assign it to the latest period possible. The poems were licensed by Milton's old friend, Thomas Tomkyns, July 2, 1670, but did not appear until 1671. They were published in the same volume, but with distinct title-pages and paginations; the publisher was John Starkey; the printer an anonymous "J.M.," who was far from equalling Symmons in elegance and correctness.

"Paradise Regained" is in one point of view the confutation of a celebrated but eccentric definition of poetry as a "criticism of life." If this were true it would be a greater work than "Paradise Lost," which must be violently strained to admit a definition not wholly inapplicable to the minor poem. If, again, Wordsworth and Coleridge are right in pronouncing "Paradise Regained" the most perfect of Milton's works in point of execution, the proof is afforded that perfect execution is not the chief test of poetic excellence. Whatever these great men may have propounded in theory, it cannot be believed that they would not have rather written the first two books of "Paradise Lost" than ten such poems as "Paradise Regained," and yet they affirm that Milton's power is even more advantageously exhibited in the latter work than in the other. There can be no solution except that greatness in poetry depends mainly upon the subject, and that the subject of "Paradise Lost" is infinitely the finer. Perhaps this should not be. Perhaps to "the visual nerve purged with euphrasy and rue" the spectacle of the human soul successfully resisting supernatural temptation would be more impressive than the material sublimities of "Paradise Lost," but ordinary vision sees otherwise. Satan "floating many a rood" on the sulphurous lake, or "up to the fiery concave towering high," or confronting Death at the gate of Hell, kindles the imagination with quite other fire than the sage circumspection and the meek fortitude of the Son of God. "The reason," says Blake, "why Milton wrote in fetters when he wrote of Angels and God, and at liberty when of Devils and Hell, is because he was a true Poet, and of the Devil's party without knowing it." The passages in "Paradise Regained" which most nearly approach the magnificence of "Paradise Lost," are those least closely connected with the proper action of the poem, the episodes with which Milton's consummate art and opulent fancy have veiled the bareness of his subject. The description of the Parthian military expedition; the picture, equally gorgeous and accurate, of the Roman Empire at the zenith of its greatness; the condensation into a single speech of all that has made Greece dear to humanity--these are the shining peaks of the regained "Paradise," marvels of art and eloquence, yet, unlike "Paradise Lost," beautiful rather than awful. The faults inherent in the theme cannot be imputed to the poet. No human skill could make the second Adam as great an object of sympathy as the first: it is enough, and it is wonderful, that spotless virtue should be so entirely exempt from formality and dulness. The baffled Satan, beaten at his own weapons, is necessarily a much less interesting personage than the heroic adventurer of "Paradise Lost." Milton has done what can be done by softening Satan's reprobate mood with exquisite strokes of pathos:--

> "Though I have lost
> Much lustre of my native brightness, lost
> To be beloved of God, I have not lost
> To love, at least contemplate and admire
> What I see excellent in good or fair,
> Or virtuous; I should so have lost all sense."

These words, though spoken with a deceitful intention, express a truth. Milton's Satan is a long way from Goethe's Mephistopheles. Profound, too, is the pathos of--

"I would be at the worst, worst is my best,
My harbour, and my ultimate repose."

The general sobriety of the style of "Paradise Regained" is a fertile theme for the critics. It is, indeed, carried to the verge of baldness; frigidity, used by Pattison, is too strong a word. This does not seem to be any token of a decay of poetical power. As writers advance in life their characteristics usually grow upon them, and develop into mannerisms. In "Paradise Regained," and yet more markedly in "Samson Agonistes," Milton seems to have prided himself on showing how independent he could be of the ordinary poetical stock-in-trade. Except in his splendid episodical descriptions he seeks to impress by the massy substance of his verse. It is a great proof of the essentially poetical quality of his mind that though he thus often becomes jejune, he is never prosaic. He is ever unmistakably the poet, even when his beauties are rather those of the orator or the moralist. The following sound remark, for instance, would not have been poetry in Pope; it is poetry in Milton:--

"Who reads
Incessantly, and to his reading brings not
A spirit and judgment equal or superior
(And what he brings what need he elsewhere seek?)
Uncertain and unsettled still remains?
Deep versed in books and shallow in himself."

Perhaps, too, the sparse flowers of pure poetry are more exquisite from their contrast with the general austerity:--

"The field, all iron, cast a gleaming brown."

"Morning fair

Came forth with pilgrim steps in amice gray."
Poetic magic these, and Milton is still Milton.

"I have lately read his Samson, which has more of the antique spirit than any production of any other modern poet. He is very great." Thus Goethe to Eckermann, in his old age. The period of life is noticeable, for "Samson Agonistes" is an old man's poem as respects author and reader alike. There is much to repel, little to attract a young reader; no wonder that Macaulay, fresh from college, put it so far below "Comus," to which the more mature taste is disposed to equal it. It is related to the earlier work as sculpture is to painting, but sculpture of the severest school, all sinewy strength; studious, above all, of impressive truth. "Beyond these an ancient fisherman and a rock are fashioned, a rugged rock, whereon with might and main the old man drags a great net from his cast, as one that labours stoutly. Thou wouldest say that he is fishing with all the might of his limbs, so big the sinews swell all about his neck, grey-haired though he is, but his strength is as the strength of youth."[9] Behold here the Milton of "Samson Agonistes," a work whose beauty is of metal rather than of marble, hard, bright, and receptive of an ineffaceable die. The great fault is the frequent harshness of the style, principally in the choruses, where some strophes are almost uncouth. In the blank verse speeches perfect grace is often united to perfect dignity: as in the farewell of Dalila:--

"Fame if not double-faced is double-mouthed,
And with contrary blast proclaims most deeds;
On both his wings, one black, the other white,
Bears greatest names in his wild aery flights.
My name perhaps among the circumcised,
In Dan, in Judah, and the bordering tribes,
To all posterity may stand defamed,
With malediction mentioned, and the blot
Of falsehood most unconjugal traduced.
But in my country where I most desire,
In Ecron, Gaza, Asdod, and in Gath,
I shall be named among the famousest

Of women, sung at solemn festivals,
Living and dead recorded, who to save
Her country from a fierce destroyer, chose
Above the faith of wedlock-bands; my tomb
With odours visited and annual flowers."

The scheme of "Samson Agonistes" is that of the Greek drama, the only one appropriate to an action of such extreme simplicity, admitting so few personages, and these only as foils to the hero. It is, but for its Miltonisms of style and autobiographic and political allusion, just such a drama as Sophocles or Euripides would have written on the subject, and has all that depth of patriotic and religious sentiment which made the Greek drama so inexpressibly significant to Greeks. Consummate art is shown in the invention of the Philistine giant, Harapha, who not only enriches the meagre action, and brings out strong features in the character of Samson, but also prepares the reader for the catastrophe. We must say reader, for though the drama might conceivably be acted with effect on a Court or University stage, the real living theatre has been no place for it since the days of Greece. Milton confesses as much when in his preface he assails "the poet's error of intermixing comic stuff with tragic sadness and gravity; or introducing trivial and vulgar persons, which by all judicious hath been counted absurd; and brought in without discretion, corruptly to gratify the people." In his view tragedy should be eclectic; in Shakespeare's it should be all embracing. Shelley, perhaps, judged more rightly than either when he said: "The modern practice of blending comedy with tragedy is undoubtedly an extension of the dramatic circle; but the comedy should be as in 'King Lear,' universal, ideal, and sublime." On the whole, "Samson Agonistes" is a noble example of a style which we may hope will in no generation be entirely lacking to our literature, but which must always be exotic, from its want of harmony with the more essential characteristics of our tumultous, undisciplined, irrepressible national life.

In one point of view, however, "Samson Agonistes" deserves to be esteemed a national poem, pregnant with a deeper allusiveness than has always been recognized. Samson's impersonation of the author himself can escape no one. Old, blind, captive, helpless, mocked, decried, miserable in the failure of all his ideals, upheld only by faith and his own unconquerable spirit, Milton is the counterpart of his hero. Particular references to the circumstances of his life are not wanting: his bitter self-condemnation for having chosen his first wife in the camp of the enemy, and his surprise that near the close of an austere life he should be afflicted by the malady appointed to chastise intemperance. But, as in the Hebrew prophets Israel sometimes denotes a person, sometimes a nation, Samson seems no less the representative of the English people in the age of Charles the Second. His heaviest burden is his remorse, a remorse which could not weigh on Milton:--

"I do acknowledge and confess
That I this honour, I this pomp have brought
To Dagon, and advanced his praises high
Among the heathen round; to God have brought
Dishonour, obloquy, and oped the mouths
Of idolists and atheists; have brought scandal
To Israel, diffidence of God, and doubt
In feeble hearts, propense enough before
To waver, to fall off, and join with idols;
Which is my chief affliction, shame, and sorrow,
The anguish of my soul, that suffers not
My eye to harbour sleep, or thoughts to rest."

Milton might reproach himself for having taken a Philistine wife, but not with having suffered her to shear him. But the same could not be said of the English nation, which had in his view most foully apostatized from its pure creed, and most perfidiously betrayed the high commission it had received from Heaven. "This extolled and magnified nation, regardless both of honour won, or deliverances vouchsafed, to fall back, or rather to creep back, so poorly as it seems the multitude would, to their once abjured and detested thraldom of kingship! To be ourselves the slanderers of our own just and religious deeds! To verify all the bitter predictions of our triumphing enemies, who will now think they wisely discerned and justly censured us and all our actions as rash, rebellious, hypocritical, and impious!" These things, which Milton refused to contemplate as possible when he wrote his "Ready Way to establish a Free Commonwealth," had actually come to pass. The English nation is to him the enslaved and erring Samson--a Samson, however, yet to burst his bonds, and bring down ruin upon Philistia. "Samson Agonistes" is thus a prophetic drama, the English counterpart of the world-drama of "Prometheus Bound."

Goethe says that our final impression of any one is derived from the last circumstances in which we have beheld him. Let us, therefore, endeavour to behold Milton as he appeared about the time of the publication of his last poems, to which period of his life the descriptions we possess seem to apply. Richardson heard of his sitting habitually "in a grey coarse cloth coat at the door of his house near Bunhill Fields, in warm sunny weather to enjoy the fresh air"--a suggestive picture. What thoughts must have been travelling through his mind, undisturbed by external things! How many of the passers knew that they flitted past the greatest glory of the age of Newton, Locke, and Wren? For one who would reverence the author of "Paradise Lost," there were probably twenty who would have been ready with a curse for the apologist of the killing of the King. In-doors he was seen by Dr. Wright, in Richardson's time an aged clergyman in Dorsetshire, who found him up one pair of stairs, in a room hung with rusty green "sitting in an elbow chair, black clothes, and neat enough, pale but not cadaverous; his hands and fingers gouty and with chalk-stones." Gout was the enemy of Milton's latter days; we have seen that he had begun to suffer from it before he wrote "Samson Agonistes." Without it, he said, he could find blindness tolerable. Yet even in the fit he would be cheerful, and would sing. It is grievous to write that, about 1670, the departure of his daughters promoted the comfort of his household. They were sent out to learn embroidery as a means of future support--a proper step in itself, and one which would appear to have entailed considerable expense upon Milton. But they might perfectly well have remained inmates of the family, and the inference is that domestic discord had at length grown unbearable to all. Friends, or at least visitors, were, on the other hand, more numerous than of late years. The most interesting were the "subtle, cunning, and reserved" Earl of Anglesey, who must have "coveted Milton's society and converse" very much if, as Phillips reports, he often came all the way to Bunhill Fields to enjoy it; and Dryden, whose generous admiration does not seem to have been affected by Milton's over-hasty sentence upon him as "a good rhymester, but no poet." One of Dryden's visits is famous in literary history, when he came with the modest request that Milton would let him turn his epic into an opera. "Aye," responded Milton, equal to the occasion, "tag my verses if you will"--to tag being to put a shining metal point--compared in Milton's fancy to a rhyme--at the end of a lace or cord. Dryden took him at his word, and in due time "Paradise Lost" had become an opera under the title of "The State of Innocence and Fall of Man," which may also be interpreted as referring to the condition of the poem before Dryden laid hands upon it and afterwards. It is a puzzling performance altogether; one sees not any more than Sir Walter Scott could see how a drama requiring paradisiacal costume could have been acted even in the age of Nell Gwyn; and yet it is even more unlikely that Dryden should have written a play not intended for the stage. The same contradiction prevails in the piece itself; it would not be unfair to call it the most absurd burlesque ever written without burlesque intention; and yet it displays such intellectual resources, such vigour, bustle, adroitness, and bright impudence, that admiration almost counterweighs derision. Dryden could not have made such an exhibition of Milton and himself twenty years afterwards, when he said that, much as he had always admired Milton, he felt that he had not admired him half enough. The reverence which he felt even in 1674 for "one of the greatest, most noble, and most sublime poems which either this age or nation has produced," contrasts finely with the ordinary Restoration estimate of Milton conveyed in the complimentary verses by Lee, prefixed to "The State of Innocence":--

"To the dead bard your fame a little owes,
For Milton did the wealthy mine disclose,
And rudely cast what you could well dispose.
He roughly drew, on an old-fashioned ground,
A chaos, for no perfect world was found,
Till through the heap your mighty genius shined;
He was the golden ore, which you refined."

These later years also produced several little publications of Milton's own, mostly of manuscripts long lying by him, now slightly revised and fitted for the press. Such were his miniature Latin grammar, published in 1669; and his "Artis Logicae Plenior Institutio; or The Method of Ramus," 1672. The first is insignificant; and the second even Professor Masson pronounces, "as a digest of logic, disorderly and unedifying." Both apparently belong to his school-keeping days: the little tract, "Of True Religion, Heresy, Schism, Toleration," (1673) is, on the other hand, contemporary with a period of great public excitement, when Parliament (March, 1673) compelled the king to revoke his edict of toleration autocratically promulgated in the preceding year, and to assent to a severe Test Act against Roman Catholics. The good sense and good nature which inclined Charles to toleration were unfortunately alloyed with less creditable motives. Protestants justly suspected him of insidiously aiming at the re-establishment of Roman Catholicism, and even the persecuted Nonconformists patriotically joined with High Churchmen to adjourn their own deliverance until the country should be safe from the common enemy. The wisdom and necessity of this course were abundantly evinced under the next reign, and while we must regret that Milton contributed his superfluous aid to restrictions only defensible on the ground of expediency, we must admit that he could not well avoid making Roman Catholics an exception to the broad tolerance he claims for all denominations of Protestants. And, after all, has not the Roman Catholic Church's notion of tolerance always been that which Macaulay imputes to Southey, that everybody should tolerate her, and that she should tolerate nobody?

A more important work, though scarcely worthy of Milton's industry, was his "History of Britain" (1670). This was a comparatively early labour, four of the six books having been written before he entered upon the Latin Secretaryship, and two under the Commonwealth. From its own point of view, this is a meritorious performance, making no pretensions to the character of a philosophical history, but a clear, easy narrative, sometimes interrupted by sententious disquisition, of transactions down to the Conquest. Like Grote, though not precisely for the same reason, Milton hands down picturesque legendary matter as he finds it, and it is to those who would see English history in its romantic aspect that, in these days of exact research, his work is chiefly to be recommended. It is also memorable for what he never saw himself, the engraved portrait, after Faithorne's crayon sketch.

"No one," says Professor Masson, "can desire a more impressive and authentic portrait of Milton in his later life. The face is such as has been given to no other human being; it was and is uniquely Milton's. Underneath the broad forehead and arched temples there

are the great rings of eye-socket, with the blind, unblemished
eyes in them, drawn straight upon you by your voice, and
speculating who and what you are; there is a severe composure in
the beautiful oval of the whole countenance, disturbed only by the
singular pouting of the rich mouth; and the entire expression is
that of English intrepidity mixed with unutterable sorrow."

Milton's care to set his house in order extended to his poetical writings. In
1673 the poems published in 1645, both English and Latin, appeared in a second
edition, disclosing *novas frondes* in one or two of Milton's earliest unprinted poems, and such of the sonnets as political considerations did not exclude; and *non
sua poma* in the Tractate of Education, curiously grafted on at the end. An even
more important publication was the second edition of "Paradise Lost" (1674) with
the original ten books for the first time divided into twelve as we now have them.
Nor did this exhaust the list of Milton's literary undertakings. He was desirous of
giving to the world his correspondence when Latin Secretary, and the "Treatise on
Christian Doctrine" which had employed so much of his thoughts at various periods
of his life. The Government, though allowing the publication of his familiar Latin
correspondence (1674), would not tolerate the letters he had written as secretary
to the Commonwealth, and the "Treatise on Christian Doctrine" was still less likely
to propitiate the licenser. Holland was in that day the one secure asylum of free
thought, and thither, in 1675, the year following Milton's death, the manuscripts
were taken or sent by Daniel Skinner, a nephew of Cyriack's, to Daniel Elzevir, who
agreed to publish them. Before publication could take place, however, a clandestine
but correct edition of the State letters appeared in London, probably by the agency
of Edward Phillips. Skinner, in his vexation, appealed to the authorities to suppress
this edition: they took the hint, and suppressed his instead. Elzevir delivered up
the manuscripts, which the Secretary of State pigeon-holed until their existence
was forgotten. At last, in 1823, Mr. Robert Lemon, rummaging in the State Paper
Office, came upon the identical parcel addressed by Elzevir to Daniel Skinner's
father which contained his son's transcript of the State Letters and the "Treatise
on Christian Doctrine." Times had changed, and the heretical work was edited and
translated by George the Fourth's favourite chaplain, and published at his Majesty's

expense.

The "Treatise on Christian Doctrine" is by far the most remarkable of all Milton's later prose publications, and would have exerted a great influence on opinion if it had appeared when the author designed. Milton's name would have been a tower of strength to the liberal eighteenth-century clergy inside and outside the Establishment. It should indeed have been sufficiently manifest that "Paradise Lost" could not have been written by a Trinitarian or a Calvinist; but theological partisanship is even slower than secular partisanship to see what it does not choose to see; and Milton's Arianism was not generally admitted until it was here avouched under his own hand. The general principle of the book is undoubting reliance on the authority of Scripture, with which such an acquaintance is manifested as could only have been gained by years of intense study. It is true that the doctrine of the inward light as the interpreter of Scripture is asserted with equal conviction; but practically this illumination seems seldom to have guided Milton to any sense but the most obvious. Hence, with the intrepid consistency that belongs to him, he is not only an Arian, but a tolerator of polygamy, finding that practice nowhere condemned in Scripture, but even recommended by respectable examples; an Anthropomorphist, who takes the ascription of human passion to the Deity in the sense certainly intended by those who made it; a believer in the materiality and natural mortality of the soul, and in the suspension of consciousness between death and the resurrection. Where less fettered by the literal Word he thinks boldly; unable to conceive creation out of nothing, he regards all existence as an emanation from the Deity, thus entitling himself to the designation of Pantheist. He reiterates his doctrine of divorce; and is as strong an Anti-Sabbatarian as Luther himself. On the Atonement and Original Sin, however, he is entirely Evangelical; and he commends public worship so long as it is not made a substitute for spiritual religion. Liturgies are evil, and tithes abominable. His exposition of social duty tempers Puritan strictness with Cavalier high-breeding, and the urbanity of a man of the world. Of his motives for publication and method of composition he says:--

> "It is with a friendly and benignant feeling towards mankind that
> I give as wide a circulation as possible to what I esteem my best
> and richest possession.... And whereas the greater part of those

who have written most largely on these subjects have been wont to
fill whole pages with explanations of their own opinions,
thrusting into the margin the texts in support of their doctrines,
I have chosen, on the contrary, to fill my pages even to
redundance with quotations from Scripture, so that as little space
as possible might be left for my own words, even when they arise
from the context of revelation itself."

There is consequently little scope for eloquence in a treatise consisting to so large an extent of quotations; but it is pervaded by a moral sublimity, more easily felt than expressed. Particular opinions will be diversely judged; but if anything could increase our reverence for Milton it would be that his last years should have been devoted to a labour so manifestly inspired by disinterested benevolence and hazardous love of truth.

His life's work was now finished, and finished with entire success as far as depended upon his own will and power. He had left nothing unwritten, nothing undone, nor was he ignorant what manner of monument he had raised for himself, It was only the condition of the State that afflicted him, and this, looking forward, he saw in more gloomy colours than it appears to us who look back. Had he attained his father's age his apprehensions would have been dispelled by the Revolution: but he had evidently for some time past been older in constitution than in years. In July, 1674, he was anticipating death; but about the middle of October, "he was very merry and seemed to be in good health of body." Early in November "the gout struck in," and he died on November 8th, late at night, "with so little pain that the time of his expiring was not perceived by those in the room." On November 12th, "all his learned and great friends in London, not without a concourse of the vulgar, accompanied his body to the church of St. Giles, near Cripplegate, where he was buried in the chancel." In 1864, the church was restored in honour of the great enemy of religious establishments. "The animosities die, but the humanities live for ever."

*   *   *   *   *

Milton's resources had been greatly impaired in his latter years by losses, and the expense of providing for his daughters. He nevertheless left, exclusive of household goods, about L900, which, by a nuncupative will made in July, 1674, he had wholly bequeathed to his wife. His daughters, he told his brother Christopher (now a Roman Catholic, and on the road to become one of James the Second's judges, but always on friendly terms with John), had been undutiful, and he thought that he had done enough for them. They naturally thought otherwise, and threatened litigation. The interrogatories administered on this occasion afford the best clue to the condition of Milton's affairs and household. At length the dispute was compromised, the nuncupative will, a kind of document always regarded with suspicion, was given up, and the widow received two-thirds of the estate instead of the whole, probably the fairest settlement that could have been arrived at. After residing some years in London she retired to Nantwich in her native county, where divers glimpses reveal her as leading the decent existence of a poor but comfortable gentlewoman as late as August or September, 1727. The inventory of her effects, amounting to L38 8s. 4d., is preserved, and includes: "Mr. Milton's pictures and coat of arms, valued at ten guineas;" and "two Books of Paradise," valued at ten shillings. Of the daughters, Anne married "a master-builder," and died in childbirth some time before 1678; Mary was dead when Phillips wrote in 1694; and Deborah survived until August 24, 1727, dying within a few days of her stepmother. She had married Abraham Clarke, a weaver and mercer in Dublin, who took refuge in England during the Irish troubles under James the Second, and carried on his business in Spitalfields. She had several children by him, one of whom lived to receive, in 1750, the proceeds of a theatrical benefit promoted by Bishop Newton and Samuel Johnson. Deborah herself was brought into notice by Addison, and was visited by Professor Ward of Gresham College, who found her "bearing the inconveniences of a low fortune with decency and prudence." Her last days were made comfortable by the generosity of Princess Caroline and others: it is more pleasant still to know that her affection for her father had revived. When shown Faithorne's crayon portrait (not the one engraved in Milton's lifetime, but one exceedingly like it) she exclaimed, "in a transport, ''Tis my dear father, I see him, 'tis him!' and then she put her hands to several parts of her face, ''Tis the very man, here! here!'"

*   *   *   *   *

Milton's character is one of the things which "securus judicat orbis terrarum." On one point only there seems to us, as we have frequently implied, to be room for modification. In the popular conception of Milton the poet and the man are imperfectly combined. We allow his greatness as a poet, but deny him the poetical temperament which alone could have enabled him to attain it. He is looked upon as a great, good, reverend, austere, not very amiable, and not very sensitive man. The author and the book are thus set at variance, and the attempt to conceive the character as a whole results in confusion and inconsistency. To us, on the contrary, Milton, with all his strength of will and regularity of life, seems as perfect a representative as any of his compeers of the sensitiveness and impulsive passion of the poetical temperament. We appeal to his remarkable dependence upon external prompting for his compositions; to the rapidity of his work under excitement, and his long intervals of unproductiveness; to the heat and fury of his polemics; to the simplicity with which, fortunately for us, he inscribes small particulars of his own life side by side with weightiest utterances on Church and State; to the amazing precipitancy of his marriage and its rupture; to his sudden pliability upon appeal to his generosity; to his romantic self-sacrifice when his country demanded his eyes from him; above all, to his splendid ideals of regenerated human life, such as poets alone either conceive or realize. To overlook all this is to affirm that Milton wrote great poetry without being truly a poet. One more remark may be added, though not required by thinking readers. We must beware of confounding the essential with the accidental Milton--the pure vital spirit with the casual vesture of the creeds and circumstances of the era in which it became clothed with mortality:--

"They are still immortal
Who, through birth's orient portal
And death's dark chasm hurrying to and fro,
Clothe their unceasing flight

In the brief dust and light
Gathered around their chariots as they go.
New shapes they still may weave,
New gods, new laws, receive."

If we knew for certain which of the many causes that have enlisted noble minds in our age would array Milton's spirit "in brief dust and light," supposing it returned to earth in this nineteenth century, we should know which was the noblest of them all, but we should be as far as ever from knowing a final and stereotyped Milton.

NOTES

[1: A famous Presbyterian tract of the day, so called from the combined initials of the authors, one of whom was Milton's old instructor, Thomas Young. The "Remonstrant" to whom Milton replied was Bishop Hall.]

[2: This principle admitted of general application. For example, astrological books were to be licensed by John Booker, who could by no means see his way to pass the prognostications of his rival Lilly without "many impertinent obliterations," which made Lilly exceeding wroth.]

[3: Two persons of this uncommon name are mentioned in the State Papers of Milton's time--one a merchant who imported a cargo of timber; the other a leatherseller. The name also occurs once in Pepys.]

[4: Rossetti's sonnet, "On the Refusal of Aid between Nations," is an almost equally remarkable instance.]

[5: The same is recorded of Friedrich Hebbel, the most original of modern German dramatists.]

[6: In his "Urim of Conscience," 1695. This curious book contains one of the first English accounts of Buddha, whom the author calls Chacabout (Sakhya Buddha, apparently), and of the "Christians of St. John" at Bassora.]

[7: Ariosto and Marcellus Palingenius. Both these wrote before Ronsard, to whom the thought is traced by Pattison, and Valvasone, to whom Hayley deems Milton indebted for it.]

[8: We cannot agree with Mr. Edmundson that Milton was in any respect indebted to Vondel's "Adam's Banishment," published in 1664.]

[9: Theocritus, Idyll I.; Lang's translation.]

The Codes Of Hammurabi And Moses
W. W. Davies

QTY

The discovery of the Hammurabi Code is one of the greatest achievements of archaeology, and is of paramount interest, not only to the student of the Bible, but also to all those interested in ancient history...

Religion   ISBN: *1-59462-338-4*   Pages:132

MSRP $12.95

The Theory of Moral Sentiments
Adam Smith

QTY

This work from 1749. contains original theories of conscience amd moral judgment and it is the foundation for systemof morals.

Philosophy ISBN: *1-59462-777-0*   Pages:536

MSRP $19.95

Jessica's First Prayer
Hesba Stretton

QTY

In a screened and secluded corner of one of the many railway-bridges which span the streets of London there could be seen a few years ago, from five o'clock every morning until half past eight, a tidily set-out coffee-stall, consisting of a trestle and board, upon which stood two large tin cans, with a small fire of charcoal burning under each so as to keep the coffee boiling during the early hours of the morning when the work-people were thronging into the city on their way to their daily toil...

Pages:84

Childrens   ISBN: *1-59462-373-2*   *MSRP $9.95*

My Life and Work
Henry Ford

QTY

Henry Ford revolutionized the world with his implementation of mass production for the Model T automobile. Gain valuable business insight into his life and work with his own auto-biography... "We have only started on our development of our country we have not as yet, with all our talk of wonderful progress, done more than scratch the surface. The progress has been wonderful enough but..."

Pages:300

Biographies/   ISBN: *1-59462-198-5*   *MSRP $21.95*

The Art of Cross-Examination
Francis Wellman

QTY

I presume it is the experience of every author, after his first book is published upon an important subject, to be almost overwhelmed with a wealth of ideas and illustrations which could readily have been included in his book, and which to his own mind, at least, seem to make a second edition inevitable. Such certainly was the case with me; and when the first edition had reached its sixth impression in five months, I rejoiced to learn that it seemed to my publishers that the book had met with a sufficiently favorable reception to justify a second and considerably enlarged edition. ..

Pages:412

Reference   **ISBN:** *1-59462-647-2*   *MSRP $19.95*

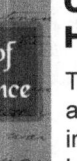

On the Duty of Civil Disobedience
Henry David Thoreau

QTY

Thoreau wrote his famous essay, On the Duty of Civil Disobedience, as a protest against an unjust but popular war and the immoral but popular institution of slave-owning. He did more than write—he declined to pay his taxes, and was hauled off to gaol in consequence. Who can say how much this refusal of his hastened the end of the war and of slavery ?

Law   **ISBN:** *1-59462-747-9*   **Pages:48**

MSRP $7.45

Dream Psychology Psychoanalysis for Beginners
Sigmund Freud

QTY

Sigmund Freud, born Sigismund Schlomo Freud (May 6, 1856 - September 23, 1939), was a Jewish-Austrian neurologist and psychiatrist who co-founded the psychoanalytic school of psychology. Freud is best known for his theories of the unconscious mind, especially involving the mechanism of repression; his redefinition of sexual desire as mobile and directed towards a wide variety of objects; and his therapeutic techniques, especially his understanding of transference in the therapeutic relationship and the presumed value of dreams as sources of insight into unconscious desires.

Pages:196

Psychology   **ISBN:** *1-59462-905-6*   *MSRP $15.45*

The Miracle of Right Thought
Orison Swett Marden

QTY

Believe with all of your heart that you will do what you were made to do. When the mind has once formed the habit of holding cheerful, happy, prosperous pictures, it will not be easy to form the opposite habit. It does not matter how improbable or how far away this realization may see, or how dark the prospects may be, if we visualize them as best we can, as vividly as possible, hold tenaciously to them and vigorously struggle to attain them, they will gradually become actualized, realized in the life. But a desire, a longing without endeavor, a yearning abandoned or held indifferently will vanish without realization.

Pages:360

Self Help   **ISBN:** *1-59462-644-8*   *MSRP $25.45*

www.bookjungle.com *email: sales@bookjungle.com fax: 630-214-0564 mail: Book Jungle PO Box 2226 Champaign, IL 61825*

QTY

The Rosicrucian Cosmo-Conception Mystic Christianity *by Max Heindel*　ISBN: *1-59462-188-8*　**$38.95**
The Rosicrucian Cosmo-conception is not dogmatic, neither does it appeal to any other authority than the reason of the student. It is: not controversial, but is: sent forth in the, hope that it may help to clear...　New Age/Religion Pages 646

Abandonment To Divine Providence *by Jean-Pierre de Caussade*　ISBN: *1-59462-228-0*　**$25.95**
"The Rev. Jean Pierre de Caussade was one of the most remarkable spiritual writers of the Society of Jesus in France in the 18th Century. His death took place at Toulouse in 1751. His works have gone through many editions and have been republished...　Inspirational/Religion Pages 400

Mental Chemistry *by Charles Haanel*　ISBN: *1-59462-192-6*　**$23.95**
Mental Chemistry allows the change of material conditions by combining and appropriately utilizing the power of the mind. Much like applied chemistry creates something new and unique out of careful combinations of chemicals the mastery of mental chemistry...　New Age Pages 354

The Letters of Robert Browning and Elizabeth Barret Barrett 1845-1846 vol II　ISBN: *1-59462-193-4*　**$35.95**
by Robert Browning and Elizabeth Barrett
Biographies Pages 596

Gleanings In Genesis (volume I) *by Arthur W. Pink*　ISBN: *1-59462-130-6*　**$27.45**
Appropriately has Genesis been termed "the seed plot of the Bible" for in it we have, in germ form, almost all of the great doctrines which are afterwards fully developed in the books of Scripture which follow...　Religion/Inspirational Pages 420

The Master Key *by L. W. de Laurence*　ISBN: *1-59462-001-6*　**$30.95**
In no branch of human knowledge has there been a more lively increase of the spirit of research during the past few years than in the study of Psychology, Concentration and Mental Discipline. The requests for authentic lessons in Thought Control, Mental Discipline and...　New Age/Business Pages 422

The Lesser Key Of Solomon Goetia *by L. W. de Laurence*　ISBN: *1-59462-092-X*　**$9.95**
This translation of the first book of the "Lemegton" which is now for the first time made accessible to students of Talismanic Magic was done, after careful collation and edition, from numerous Ancient Manuscripts in Hebrew, Latin, and French...　New Age/Occult Pages 92

Rubaiyat Of Omar Khayyam *by Edward Fitzgerald*　ISBN:*1-59462-332-5*　**$13.95**
Edward Fitzgerald, whom the world has already learned, in spite of his own efforts to remain within the shadow of anonymity, to look upon as one of the rarest poets of the century, was born at Bredfield, in Suffolk, on the 31st of March, 1809. He was the third son of John Purcell...　Music Pages 172

Ancient Law *by Henry Maine*　ISBN: *1-59462-128-4*　**$29.95**
The chief object of the following pages is to indicate some of the earliest ideas of mankind, as they are reflected in Ancient Law, and to point out the relation of those ideas to modern thought.　Religiom/History Pages 452

Far-Away Stories *by William J. Locke*　ISBN: *1-59462-129-2*　**$19.45**
"Good wine needs no bush, but a collection of mixed vintages does. And this book is just such a collection. Some of the stories I do not want to remain buried for over in the museum files of dead magazine-numbers un author's not unpardonable vanity..."　Fiction Pages 272

Life of David Crockett *by David Crockett*　ISBN: *1-59462-250-7*　**$27.45**
"Colonel David Crockett was one of the most remarkable men of the times in which he lived. Born in humble life, but gifted with a strong will, an indomitable courage, and unremitting perseverance...　Biographies/New Age Pages 424

Lip-Reading *by Edward Nitchie*　ISBN: *1-59462-206-X*　**$25.95**
Edward B. Nitchie, founder of the New York School for the Hard of Hearing, now the Nitchie School of Lip-Reading, Inc, wrote "LIP-READING Principles and Practice". The development and perfecting of this meritorious work on lip-reading was an undertaking...　How-to Pages 400

A Handbook of Suggestive Therapeutics, Applied Hypnotism, Psychic Science　ISBN: *1-59462-214-0*　**$24.95**
by Henry Munro
Health/New Age/Health/Self-help Pages 376

A Doll's House: and Two Other Plays *by Henrik Ibsen*　ISBN: *1-59462-112-8*　**$19.95**
Henrik Ibsen created this classic when in revolutionary 1848 Rome. Introducing some striking concepts in playwriting for the realist genre, this play has been studied the world over.　Fiction/Classics/Plays 308

The Light of Asia *by sir Edwin Arnold*　ISBN: *1-59462-204-3*　**$13.95**
In this poetic masterpiece, Edwin Arnold describes the life and teachings of Buddha. The man who was to become known as Buddha to the world was born as Prince Gautama of India but he rejected the worldly riches and abandoned the reigns of power when...　Religion/History/Biographies Pages 170

The Complete Works of Guy de Maupassant *by Guy de Maupassant*　ISBN: *1-59462-157-8*　**$16.95**
"For days and days, nights and nights, I had dreamed of that first kiss which was to consecrate our engagement, and I knew not on what spot I should put my lips..."　Fiction/Classics Pages 240

The Art of Cross-Examination *by Francis L. Wellman*　ISBN: *1-59462-309-0*　**$26.95**
Written by a renowned trial lawyer, Wellman imparts his experience and uses case studies to explain how to use psychology to extract desired information through questioning.　How-to/Science/Reference Pages 408

Answered or Unanswered? *by Louisa Vaughan*　ISBN: *1-59462-248-5*　**$10.95**
Miracles of Faith in China
Religion Pages 112

The Edinburgh Lectures on Mental Science (1909) *by Thomas*　ISBN: *1-59462-008-3*　**$11.95**
This book contains the substance of a course of lectures recently given by the writer in the Queen Street Hall, Edinburgh. Its purpose is to indicate the Natural Principles governing the relation between Mental Action and Material Conditions...　New Age/Psychology Pages 148

Ayesha *by H. Rider Haggard*　ISBN: *1-59462-301-5*　**$24.95**
Verily and indeed it is the unexpected that happens! Probably if there was one person upon the earth from whom the Editor of this, and of a certain previous history, did not expect to hear again...　Classics Pages 380

Ayala's Angel *by Anthony Trollope*　ISBN: *1-59462-352-X*　**$29.95**
The two girls were both pretty, but Lucy who was twenty-one who supposed to be simple and comparatively unattractive, whereas Ayala was credited, as her Bombwhat romantic name might show, with poetic charm and a taste for romance. Ayala when her father died was nineteen...　Fiction Pages 484

The American Commonwealth *by James Bryce*　ISBN: *1-59462-286-8*　**$34.45**
An interpretation of American democratic political theory. It examines political mechanics and society from the perspective of Scotsman James Bryce　Politics Pages 572

Stories of the Pilgrims *by Margaret P. Pumphrey*　ISBN: *1-59462-116-2*　**$17.95**
This book explores pilgrims religious oppression in England as well as their escape to Holland and eventual crossing to America on the Mayflower, and their early days in New England...　History Pages 268

www.bookjungle.com *email: sales@bookjungle.com fax: 630-214-0564 mail: Book Jungle PO Box 2226 Champaign, IL 61825*

QTY

The Fasting Cure *by Sinclair Upton*   ISBN: *1-59462-222-1*   **$13.95**
In the Cosmopolitan Magazine for May, 1910, and in the Contemporary Review (London) for April, 1910, I published an article dealing with my experiences in fasting. I have written a great many magazine articles, but never one which attracted so much attention... New Age/Self Help/Health Pages 164

Hebrew Astrology *by Sepharial*   ISBN: *1-59462-308-2*   **$13.45**
In these days of advanced thinking it is a matter of common observation that we have left many of the old landmarks behind and that we are now pressing forward to greater heights and to a wider horizon than that which represented the mind-content of our progenitors... Astrology Pages 144

Thought Vibration or The Law of Attraction in the Thought World   ISBN: *1-59462-127-6*   **$12.95**
by William Walker Atkinson   *Psychology/Religion Pages 144*

Optimism *by Helen Keller*   ISBN: *1-59462-108-X*   **$15.95**
Helen Keller was blind, deaf, and mute since 19 months old, yet famously learned how to overcome these handicaps, communicate with the world, and spread her lectures promoting optimism. An inspiring read for everyone... Biographies/Inspirational Pages 84

Sara Crewe *by Frances Burnett*   ISBN: *1-59462-360-0*   **$9.45**
In the first place, Miss Minchin lived in London. Her home was a large, dull, tall one, in a large, dull square, where all the houses were alike, and all the sparrows were alike, and where all the door-knockers made the same heavy sound... Childrens/Classic Pages 88

The Autobiography of Benjamin Franklin *by Benjamin Franklin*   ISBN: *1-59462-135-7*   **$24.95**
The Autobiography of Benjamin Franklin has probably been more extensively read than any other American historical work, and no other book of its kind has had such ups and downs of fortune. Franklin lived for many years in England, where he was agent... Biographies/History Pages 332

Name	
Email	
Telephone	
Address	
City, State ZIP	

☐ **Credit Card**   ☐ **Check / Money Order**

Credit Card Number	
Expiration Date	
Signature	

Please Mail to: Book Jungle
PO Box 2226
Champaign, IL 61825
or Fax to: 630-214-0564

ORDERING INFORMATION

web: *www.bookjungle.com*
email: *sales@bookjungle.com*
fax: *630-214-0564*
mail: *Book Jungle PO Box 2226 Champaign, IL 61825*
or PayPal *to sales@bookjungle.com*

Please contact us for bulk discounts

DIRECT-ORDER TERMS

20% Discount if You Order Two or More Books
Free Domestic Shipping!
Accepted: Master Card, Visa, Discover, American Express

www.ingramcontent.com/pod-product-compliance
Lightning Source LLC
Chambersburg PA
CBHW080744250626
47162CB00010B/3022